SPY TRADE

SPY TRADE

A Spycatcher Novella

MATTHEW DUNN

WITNESS
IMPULSE

An Imprint of HarperCollinsPublishers

Excerpt from *The Spy House* copyright © 2015 by Matthew Dunn.

EPub Edition AUGUST 2015 ISBN: 9780062309372

Print Edition ISBN: 9780062441423

10 9 8 7 6 5 4

To my children

CHAPTER 1

Northern Iraq

Later today, Bob Oakland would wish he'd been killed in a manner that was quick and painless and nothing like how he imagined it would feel to have the blade of a penknife saw through his gullet.

A thirty-year veteran of the CIA, Oakland was due to retire in a few months and had been told that he could complete his career with pretty much any cushy job he wanted. Most in his position would have opted for a desk job in Langley: a nine-to-five idyll with ample time to dust off bass-fishing rods and prepare them for good use in retirement. Thing was, though, Oakland still had a mind that thought it was young, and no way was it going to let him pass over the opportunity to act like Wilfred Thesiger or T. E. Lawrence and trek across a desert that was hard underfoot, mostly flat, and so hot that he could feel its heat through the soles of his shoes.

The five men with him were half Oakland's age. Four of them wore headscarves and shawls to make them look like Bedouins from a distance; though underneath the veneer of disguise they were thoroughbred Americans with military gear and weapons that were only issued to men who'd qualified to become Navy SEALs. The fifth was a Jordanian translator who was wearing jeans, a Metallica T-shirt, and Ray-Bans, and had modeled his psyche to be more American than that of anyone else in the group.

"You're going to this meeting wearing a suit?" one of the sailors had asked Oakland as they'd boarded a Chinook helicopter. "We're on foot for at least five miles once we land."

"I'm wearing a suit," Oakland had replied with a mischievous twinkle in his eyes, "because I must represent what can be."

And though it was wholly impractical, he'd worn a suit every time he'd been inserted into parts of northern Iraq and western Syria during the last few weeks. The former Istanbul station chief's assignment was to meet Shiite tribal leaders and exchange sugary tea for American dollars and guns. The leaders always gave him the warmest of embraces—not because he came bearing gifts but because he was a gentleman who was genuinely interested in them.

No doubt there were other officers in the Agency who would have been better suited to the hardships of the job. Bob kept himself fit, but long gone were the days when he could run half marathons in respectable times and win trophies for his athleticism in squash. Of medium height, and with a build that carried little fat, Bob still looked good though age was starting to make his body ache in odd places and stiffen his gait. But Bob had two things that age couldn't diminish: a razor-sharp brain and a compassion for the foreign nationals he worked with. The Agency had decided the Middle Eastern job needed a man who thought like an intelligence officer yet conducted himself as a diplomat. Bob was that man.

Today was his final foray into the wilderness. Had he made a difference? Probably, but only time would tell whether it was one for the better. So often in history, donated American guns had been turned against the men who'd delivered them; freedom fighters were rapidly recategorized as terrorists; American students would go on protest marches against their government; East and West Coast American historians and journalists would rage against yet further examples of insidious American foreign-policy blunders; and always the Agency would be blamed, as if it were an all-pervasive force of evil that just plain and simple never learned from its mistakes.

In truth, Oakland didn't care how his service would pan out in the history books. What mattered to him was that he was now doing what he reckoned Thesiger and Lawrence would be doing if they were alive today. Some might say that Oakland was a vainglorious liability who was urgently grasping a chance of unadulterated masculinity—what he did to his surroundings wasn't what mattered; it was what the surroundings did to him that had meaning. But Oakland wasn't so self-centered. On the contrary, his whole career had been one of selfless service. Postings to sweaty parts of the world; spying on the countries he worked within; processing defectors; getting married; getting divorced; getting married again; wishing he hadn't; watching others steal the glory for his clever initiatives; visitors from headquarters taking him out for boozy lunches, telling him he was doing a great job, then getting on the fastest plane back to the States; and always thinking to himself that one day his life in the CIA would be exhilarating. And therein was the problem. Bob's career had been interesting at times, for sure. But it had never been truly adventurous.

No. Oakland wasn't in the desert because he was vainglorious.

He was here because he wanted to leave the Agency with at least one exciting story to tell.

Wind blasted his face with sand. The SEALs donned goggles. Oakland placed his hand in front of his eyes, and leaned forward a bit as he trudged onward, his mind imagining his grandchildren's mouths wide open as he sat on his porch while telling them that this trek was in fact twenty miles long and bullets were whistling past them as they fearlessly moved toward their goal.

"Okay, we got it," said one of the SEALs. "Stay here while I check it out." He pulled out his carbine from underneath his shawl and jogged down an escarpment toward a distant and isolated village.

Thirty minutes later, the SEAL returned. "Seems fine. The lookout's given us the signal to proceed, plus the correct hand code that all's good."

Cautiously, they moved over the baked-clay ground and past rocky terrain toward the village. Sand clung to Oakland's sweaty face and his matted grey hair, but he didn't care because to do so would ruin this moment. This was his last adventure. Alright, bullets weren't whizzing past them, and the route here was shorter than it would be when recounting his tale, but there was one thing he wanted to be true, and that was making this final foray without complaining. If T. E. Lawrence could make the impassable Nefud Desert crossing to surprise the Turkish stronghold in Aqaba and do so without grumbling, then Oakland could darn well get to the village without looking and sounding like a sissy.

The village was mostly comprised of russet-colored stone buildings that were low in height and clustered close together. There were twenty-two of them, and they had no fortification to protect them from attack other than a wire fence that was in place to stop goats from wandering out of the encampment and dying in the scorched expanse that resembled the surface of Mars. Oakland could now hear the animals' bells clanging as the beasts trotted between buildings and their occupants. Children and women were visible, the former dressed lightly, the latter wearing headscarves and ankle-length smocks. A handful of men were on the roofs of their homes, some holding Kalashnikov rifles, others brandishing muskets that were made in the nineteenth century. They were watching the group approach their homes, but nobody in Oakland's team or in the village had weapons raised. That would have been bad manners. Good strangers arrived in places like these with their palms extended in a gesture of peace. Good villagers reciprocated by not shooting them in the head.

As they neared the wire fence, Oakland gestured for the SEALs to stop and for the translator to come with him. Both men walked up to the fence and waited.

A young man emerged from one of the huts, slung his rifle over his back, and walked quickly to the fence. The translator and villager shook hands and spoke a few words in Arabic. The villager lifted a fence post out of the ground, allowing a gap for Oakland and his team to pass through. Once inside the perimeter, the American sailors walked through the small settlement, checking for any signs that all was not well, before taking up defensive positions around the outskirts of the buildings.

"*As-salâmu alaykum,*" said the tribal elder while sitting on rugs within one of the huts.

Oakland replied, "*Wa alaykumu s-salâmu wa rabmatu l-lâhi wa barakâtuh.*"

"My friend, my friend," said the elder in English while gesturing to the floor opposite him. "Come, come."

Oakland sat. The translator joined him at his side.

"I have a few words of English, but not enough." Switching back into Arabic, the elder said, "I hear you are leaving us soon. You return to the United States of America."

The Jordanian translated the conversation.

"Where did you hear that?" asked Oakland.

The elder shrugged. "Words travel in the wind." He waved his hand impatiently at another man in the room, who quickly disappeared to make tea. "You will miss us?"

Oakland laughed. "I'll miss you people. But I'm not convinced I'll miss the desert. I don't know how you guys do it."

The tribal leader nodded. "You know why we live here?"

Oakland answered, "You live here because no one else can."

"An astute observation."

The tea arrived and was distributed to the elder and his guests.

Oakland took a sip of his drink, masking the desire to gag because the liquid was so sweet. "Looks like others think they can also live here."

"Ah, yes. Man-boys from the English city of Birmingham and other places believe the Internet can supply them with all the worldly knowledge they need; and despite never have been farther east than during school day-trips to Paris, they think their bodies and minds are strong enough to come here and establish a state of Islam." The elder grinned though his eyes were piercing. "They are children, Mr. Oakland, who don't know what to do with their desire for adventure. They would be better off joining your armies or getting drunk and having a fight."

"Get it out of their system?"

"Before becoming true men."

Oakland had never been in the military and spent more time in his late teens and early twenties reading books than propping up bars. "Not all of them are kids. There are a bunch of bona fide psychopaths in ISIS."

"Indeed there are. And they are surrounded by the armor-plated naivety of youth and their false cause." The elder lowered his head, deep in thought. "I do not dismiss them so lightly. Their tactics are barbaric but effective. They are well supplied. And they shoot with a steady hand and eye." He looked at Oakland. "My men think they are devils. That means ISIS has won half the battle before they've even engaged with us. We need your help. Good guns and equipment will steady my men's nerves."

"And that's why I'm here."

"Yet, you travel light. I see no evidence of your carrying large sacks of guns and money."

"Your friends should have told you that's not how I work."

"You are a thoughtful man?"

Oakland nodded. "I try to be." He placed his tea on the rug and wondered if the elder would notice if he didn't drink any more. "Every village is different—terrains, operating environments, population, skills or otherwise, food, crops, mobility . . . I made a decision when I took over this job that I'd give you folk what you need, not what I *think* you need. You tell me now what will help you kill ISIS, and in a couple of hours, that equipment will be air-dropped to your village."

The leader beamed. "An enlightened American."

"A practical one."

"When you return to America, what will you do?"

"Retire, get bitched at by my wife, get fat, get bitched at some more, go fishing, and drink beer."

"But you are an elder now, Mr. Oakland. You should have respect from your family and should give yourself respect."

"You have a point." Oakland took out a pen and notepad. "Tell me what you need."

The first gunshots almost certainly belonged to the SEALs' weapons.

The second volley came from the roofs of the village.

The return fire came from the distance: some of it automatic gunfire, others sounded like high-velocity sniper fire.

The elder leapt to his feet and started barking orders in Arabic as male villagers rushed into the room to usher their leader away to a part of the village where he could issue commands and be protected. But he shrugged off their hands, and asked, "How many?"

Oakland ran to the door and glanced toward the fence. A SEAL was nearby, on one knee while sending short bursts of gunfire toward the top of the escarpment. From somewhere on the rise, a flash of light preceded a thin trail of smoke that whooshed toward the village.

"Incoming," screamed the SEAL.

A second later, a missile hit the adjacent hut, causing it to tear in half and send debris toward the SEAL. The operative was lifted off the ground, most of his face traveling onward with the debris.

Oakland spun back into the room, his whole body covered in dust from the explosion. "You've got to get out of here," he shouted in English at the elder. "Evacuate the village!"

"No. We fight," replied the tribal leader, withdrawing a pistol.

Oakland talked fast to the petrified-looking translator, before concluding, "Tell him!"

The translator spoke imploringly in Arabic to the elder. "It's ISIS. You cannot be found here with Americans. Your children and women will be raped before they're executed. Your men will be slaughtered. And you, sir, won't be able to do anything about it before you are butchered. Please, get your village safe."

The leader looked defiant and was about to speak.

But Oakland grabbed his arm, not caring whether the action was disrespectful. "We're running out of time! Get your people away from here. Only come back to fight when they're safe." He heard the translator muttering Oakland's words in Arabic.

The elder kept his eyes fixed on the CIA man. In English, he said, "We'll come back and kill these dogs." He handed him his pistol. "Keep the last bullet for yourself." He left the room with his men while shouting further orders.

More rapid gunfire came from nearby, meaning some of the SEALs were still alive and engaging the enemy.

The translator looked imploringly at Oakland. "What must we do?"

Oakland ducked low as another nearby explosion tore apart a building. "Let's try to get to the south side of the village and hope that ISIS is only hitting us from one flank and that my men can hold them off."

They raced out of the hut into the center of the village. The noise of gunshots now seemed to be constant and much closer. Beyond the southern-perimeter fence, the Arab villagers were running into the desert, women clutching their children, the men covering their backs by pointing their weapons at the northern escarpment.

"Maybe we should go with them," gasped the young translator. "They know how to survive out there."

Oakland shook his head. "I gave my reasons why we can't be caught with the villagers. For them to stand a chance of living, we've got to keep away from them."

The Jordanian placed his hands onto his head. "We're going to die!"

Oakland and the translator moved to the eastern side of the village. The CIA officer exclaimed, "Shit!" when he saw another SEAL had been shot in the head and torso, his body lying at an awkward angle on the ground. In the distance, two men dressed in black combat gear approached the village. They fired their rifles; bullets ricocheted off rocks near Oakland. Bob returned fire with the elder's pistol though the encroaching men were too far away for his rounds to stand a chance of hitting them.

The two remaining SEALs moved into the center of the village; one of them was limping, his leg bloody. His able-bodied colleague sent a volley of fire toward the escarpment and ran to Oakland. He shouted above the noise, "Got two of them coming for us," he pointed, "from over there."

Oakland followed his gaze. "Another two are coming from the northeast."

"Yeah, and they've got at least one sniper and one guy with a missile launcher on high ground. Bastards are covering their pals' asses and kicking ours." The SEAL glanced around. "Where are the villagers?"

"I told them to get out of here because . . ."

"That was a good call. Listen: we'll hold ISIS off and try to take them down when they get close. You and heavy-metal dude here need to put some klicks between you and us. I'll find you if we're not dead." He ran back to his colleague, helped him prop himself up against a wall, so that he could fire his gun, and clambered onto the roof of one of the huts.

Oakland and the translator exited the village, heading southwest, away from the attacking force. Oakland had to drag his translator because the Jordanian was so petrified, his body wanted to curl into a ball. They staggered over the desert, Oakland ripping off his tie and jacket, flies jabbing his stinging eyes as the men headed across the vast expanse of godforsaken land that was permanently blowtorched by the sun. Oakland's mouth felt dry because he feared what lay behind and ahead and because he'd sweated buckets since the American helicopter had dumped him in this place.

The translator exclaimed, "We might as well surrender."

Oakland grabbed the translator and continued walking.

What was happening was nothing like the tiresome cocktail circuits in Jakarta, Managua, and Khartoum.

And it was considerably more dangerous than the exaggerated tale he'd constructed in his head to recount to offspring.

Too dangerous.

Too real.

A story he didn't want to tell.

His heart pumped so fast he thought it might explode, and in a way he hoped it would. The Jordanian's words now sounded distant and irrelevant as he put one foot in front of the other and headed toward oblivion and death. His mind now cloudy, Oakland imagined the actor Omar Sharif appearing on horseback in the heat haze on the horizon, just as he did in the movie *Lawrence of Arabia*, dressed in traditional Bedouin black garb, and dispatching the ISIS men with the dispassionate calm of a man who is indignant that a water hole is sullied by men who do not belong to his tribe.

But there was no one ahead to help Oakland and his Jordanian colleague.

And behind them, all gunshots ceased.

The two SEALs had won?

ISIS had won?

Oakland knew he would soon find out because there was no way he could walk more than a few more yards. He collapsed to the ground and sat there, patting the ground while looking at the blinding sky. He'd put his life into the CIA, and in return, the Agency had sent him to his death.

The Jordanian pushed himself off the sand and crouched before him, salty tears running down his face. "You wish to die?"

Oakland checked the pistol and saw that only one bullet

remained in the magazine. "No, I don't wish to die. I wish to turn the clock back."

Endless miles of desert lay before them. Even Lawrence wouldn't have risked that journey without a camel and Bedouins by his side. And behind them were devils.

"You got to do what's best for you," said Oakland in a gravelly voice. It made him sound profound and manly. Perhaps that was how it should end.

It didn't end that way. Men in black, who bore none of the stoicism or clinical nobility of Sharif, slammed the butts of their rifles into Oakland's jaw and the Jordanian's temple. Unconscious, the American and his friend were dragged across shingle and dust, their faces lacerated by sharp objects and melted by their heat.

ISIS had its prisoners.

Oakland would soon wish he were dead.

CHAPTER 2

Ordinarily, America's finest brains would have wondered how the collared dove had infiltrated the large operations hall within the CIA headquarters in Langley. Some of the Agency operatives within the room might have quipped that the bird didn't need to have a security pass to enter the building, get lost in the labyrinth of corridors and rooms, and settle upon the ops center as a place where it could hop and flap between computer terminals and desks and light fittings and wall-mounted frames containing TV monitors and maps. Others might have countered that the bird would need to have the ability to press the number six within the elevator to access the floor they were on. A few might have suggested the creature accessed the zone via an open window though they would be quick to dismiss the idea as impossible since all windows in the Agency are hermetically sealed.

Patrick Bolte took it upon himself to establish how the dove got in. There was only one plausible explanation—one of the eighty-plus people in the room had brought the bird to work in a container that somehow got sufficiently loose for the dove to escape.

"Where can I get some coffee?" asked Patrick of the person nearest to him.

The young analyst didn't look up. "Where everyone else gets it. Corner of the room." She was tapping fast on her keyboard, wearing an irritable expression. She glanced at him and blanched. "Sorry, sir. I didn't know it was you."

"That's okay." Patrick smiled. "This time of morning, I'm like everyone else. I just need a caffeine hit. When were you drafted in?"

"All of us were called yesterday evening. We've been working through the night."

"Sounds like you could do with the coffee more than me. Want me to make you one?"

The analyst looked embarrassed. "That's kind, but I'm fine."

"Where's Mr. Soames?"

She gestured toward the back end of the hall. "In the conference room. He's expecting you."

Patrick walked across the hall and entered the conference room.

"Ah, Patrick's graced us with his presence. That means the world can now sleep peacefully." Tom Soames looked tired and on edge. He had every reason to be as he was the head of the Agency and had lost one of his employees in Iraq.

Seated next to him at the conference table was Lieutenant General Jerry Kinnear, the head of the Joint Special Operations Command, an organization that consisted of special-missions units and experts at gathering intelligence within battle zones. Kinnear was wearing a civilian suit though he still looked every inch the military man, with black hair that had been cut short at the sides, the physique of a long-distance runner, and cheeks that were hollow from either lack of food, too much exercise, or both.

By contrast, Soames was a bear of a man, with inches of fat covering what was still a powerful and vigorous frame. He presented himself well for a man of his shape—tailored suits that were cut in such a way so as to disguise his girth; expensive haircuts, even though the central strip of his head was bare of any strands; antique reading spectacles that might have looked pretentious on most men but gave Soames the appearance of a stout professor whose acute intellect would slice in half anyone less than his cerebral equal; and cologne that was purchased and imported from Paris perfumeries.

Patrick sat on the opposite side of the table. Like Soames and Kinnear, the CIA director was middle-aged, but there the similarities ended. He was as tall as Soames though his physique was wiry and deceptively strong; his suit was immaculately pressed but not expensive, and nor did he wear it in the way the military men did while feeling that they looked like fish out of water; his full head of silver hair was cut short enough to complete his professional demeanor but long enough to make him look like a crazy man if he shook his head wildly; and Soames and Kinnear were well and truly in the public eye.

Patrick was not.

There were eight directors in the CIA who reported to Soames and who were visible in the Agency. Yet, though it was widely known within the CIA that Patrick was a very-high-ranking officer, very few knew what he did and even fewer that he was the Agency's ninth director. Patrick liked it that way. He didn't want to be visible or to put in place a career ladder that subjugated the tasks in hand in favor of groveling around the power corridors of Capitol Hill. Patrick had reached the zenith of his career, and it was a very unusual place to be.

Until it had recently been shut down, he'd been co-head of the highly secretive joint CIA-MI6 Task Force S. It had been the perfect job for a through-and-through operator as he was, one that gave him and his small force the most complex and dangerous assignments in Western Intelligence.

But now he was a director without portfolio, idling away his time while senior CIA management tried to decide what to do with him.

"Why am I here?" Patrick asked, crossing his legs and examining fingertips that had been printless ever since his hands had been forced into molten metal.

"Bob Oakland's why, and you know it," replied Soames, with no effort to hide his irritation with Patrick's question.

"Most likely he and his translator are dead."

"Not according to my men," interjected Kinnear. "I deployed a search-and-rescue unit to the village yesterday afternoon. Once the village elder was confident the women and kids were safe, he asked for six volunteers to form a raiding party and go back to the village to rescue Oakland and kill ISIS. They trekked across fourteen miles of desert. It was unbelievably courageous. The village was empty when they got there, save for the four dead SEALs and my S&R team. Then they searched the village surroundings. The raiding party told the S&R unit they were certain from tracks in the desert that Oakland and his translator had been attacked, not killed, and taken away in two vehicles."

"ISIS has taken its highest-value hostage to date."

Kinnear was motionless. "That's providing ISIS knows he's CIA."

Soames darted a look at the general. "Oakland's a Western guy in a suit, meeting a Shiite opponent of ISIS in a remote Iraqi village. ISIS knows he's CIA."

"What action have you taken?" Patrick looked at both men in turn.

"General Kinnear's in charge of trying to locate Oakland. Since Bob went missing fifteen hours ago, Kinnear's . . ."

"Increased drone and satellite surveillance over northern Iraq and western Syria, put JSOC personnel on the ground, together with seconded units from the Rangers, USAF, and CIA Special Activities Division, and I've got NSA working round the clock to try to cover ISIS comms." Kinnear prodded the table. "If Bob Oakland's out there, we'll find him."

"But the issue is whether you'll do so in time to save his life." Patrick repeated, "Why am I here?"

Kinnear laughed. "Damned if I know."

Soames replied, "The Agency—not the military—has primacy on this operation. We cannot allow Oakland to be killed. Aside from the fact that Oakland deserves far better after spending his whole career serving the CIA, an ISIS execution of a CIA officer would be a massive propaganda win for the jihadists." He wondered how he'd feel if he'd heard someone describe his imminent death as merely a *propaganda win*. "I want Bob safe."

Patrick gestured toward Kinnear. "And you're doing everything you can to achieve that."

"Really?" The head of the CIA shook his head. "I doubt that. Why do *you* think you're here?"

"Because you want to know who tipped off ISIS that Bob and his team were going to be at the village."

Soames nodded. "Someone's got loose lips."

"In the Agency?"

"Not sure." Soames pointed at Kinnear. "More likely uniform. Either way, this needs investigating by an outsider. The best of them are known to you. Have anyone in mind?"

Patrick hesitated before nodding. "I have someone."

Bob Oakland remembered a day in his childhood when he and his fellow six-year-old classmates were sent out into a bitterly cold school playground during morning break and told to play. Like him, all of the kids were wearing thick coats, some had gloves, others thrust their hands in pockets because they'd lost their mittens and were too guilt-ridden to tell their parents they'd mislaid yet another item. Nobody played. It was too cold. Instead, kids huddled in groups of four or five and whiled away the time before they could get back inside the school. It was a rare moment when all of them wanted to be in class.

The playground had metal climbing frames and painted white lines on the paved ground encouraging them to play hopscotch and compete in sports. On that day, the paintings were superfluous because nobody was inclined to risk their neck on the ice-covered surface. The kids were nevertheless bored, irascible, and wanting adventure. Some of them offered a challenge to bite an iron bar that was part of an assault course. Bob took up the challenge, partly because he too was bored and more important because he wanted to find out if it was true that his tongue would freeze to the metal.

Mitten-covered hands either side of a head that was adorned with a knitted velvet hat, Oakland gripped the four-inch-wide bar and bit. His mouth didn't freeze solid to the metal. But fingernail-sized flakes of iron entered his mouth, and they tasted of blood.

He hated the taste of iron then; and he hated it now.

As he awoke in agony—legs bruised and lashed with ropes, a face that felt squishy and throbbed, cracked ribs making breathing hell, pain that raced from his groin to his head and was no doubt related to the huge bootprint over his crotch—he wanted more than anything else for the taste of iron to go away. His mouth was filled with blood. After spitting out what he could, he looked around. A chain around his neck, fixed at one end to a wall, yanked his head back. He gasped, realizing he could move no more than a few inches from his seated position on the floor in the corner of the large room.

There was nothing in the room except Oakland, the translator, a single bulb hanging from the ceiling that cast shadowy yellow light over the windowless room, and large red Arabic letters on one of the walls. The translator was adjacent to the inscription at the far end of the room, also seated, trapped in ropes and chains. His clothes were ripped and bloody, and his bowed head was cut open at the crown, his normally coiffured black hair a crimson tangle. He wasn't moving.

Oakland called out to him in hushed volume. "Ramzi. Ramzi. Can you hear me?"

Ramzi was motionless.

"Ramzi?"

The young Jordanian slowly lifted his head. His face had clearly taken a severe beating because it was swollen, bruised, and lacerated. "Oakland," he murmured before coughing and wincing.

"Where are we?" the CIA officer asked urgently.

"Don't . . . don't know." His voice was weak. "Think they brought us here yesterday. Can't be sure."

"What happened?"

Ramzi tried to straighten his upper torso, but his chained throat suffered the same fate as Oakland's when he'd tried to move. "You can't remember?"

The last thing Bob could recall was the momentary agony of being hit in the face in the desert. "Nothing."

Ramzi stared at the closed door in the room. "I woke up while they were driving us across the desert. It was night. Fucking jeep was bouncing so hard, I vomited. That caught their attention. One of the men hit me with his gun. Passed out again."

Bob tried to keep his voice calm when he asked, "Was I in the same vehicle as you?"

"No. I spotted a second vehicle behind us when I was awake. You must have been in there."

"How many men?"

"There were three of them in my jeep." Ramzi shrugged, then gasped as his bonds cut into his body. "Guess . . . guess same number in your car."

Six ISIS men. Four of them had approached the village on foot while the fifth watched over them with a sniper rifle, and the sixth caused havoc with his missile launcher.

Ramzi lifted his hands, placed them against his injured head, and cursed when he saw his blood had coated the ropes around his wrists. "I wish they'd put a bullet in my head."

Bob Oakland didn't know what to think. He was confused, and in absolute pain; the idea of a quick and clean death was tempting though part of him still clung to the notion that he had to survive.

The door opened, and two men, both bearded, one tall, the other shorter yet with a broad and powerful physique, entered the room. They were wearing combat fatigues, boots, and holding batons. Oakland's stomach knotted; Ramzi involuntarily thrashed, the chains and ropes making him bug-eyed as they jerked him back into position.

The shorter man was silent as he unlocked the chain fixed to the wall behind Oakland and used it to drag the CIA officer to the center of the room.

"Fuck you!" Bob stared defiantly at the jihadist.

"Shut up." The taller man's English was accented. He slammed his baton into one of Bob's shins, forcing the officer onto his knees while his colleague held the chain tight so that Bob's upper torso was erect. "The more you act like a foul-mouthed infidel, the more we treat you like one."

Where had these men come from? This was something that Bob had expertise in, as he'd spent more time working overseas than in the States. They weren't Arabs; nor were they Westerners. Their faces were a little swarthy though it was hard to tell whether that was due to their ethnicity or time spent under the sun. But the man's accent was telling. Bob was certain the men were Chechen Muslims, an ethnic group that had been the scourge of the Soviet Union and, subsequently, Russia. And unlike the Western kids in ISIS that the village elder had derided, these men brought decades of combat and terrorist experience to the region. Bob dearly hoped that meant they had some degree of maturity and restraint though the look in their eyes told him it was probably a false hope. No doubt, these men were psychopaths.

Four more of them entered the room and positioned a video camera on a tripod in front of Bob. All of them donned headscarves to disguise their faces. The camera was turned on, and they stood behind Bob, the red Arabic letters on the wall clearly visible above their heads.

Bob wondered, Is this it? A knife sawed through my gullet while the camera rolls? He didn't know how he'd get through that ordeal, then realized it was a stupid thought given he'd have no choice other than to suffer whatever was dished out to him.

The tall man was probably their leader. Speaking to the camera, he said, "We have traveled to the Middle East to join Islamic State. We hope our brothers in ISIS will accept us into their ranks. But we must do something first, to prove to ISIS that we are worthy to become their warriors. This is our proof." He grabbed the chain from his colleague and pulled it back, forcing Bob's face upward. "This man is an American spy. He represents everything that is sick with the world. He will suffer"—he nodded at one of his colleagues, who swung his baton into Ramzi's arm, causing the translator to scream—"far worse than this traitor to Allah." He held a knife to Bob's throat. "America: you will do what we ask, or you will watch this pig die." The Chechen leader said to Bob, "Tell the world your name."

The CIA officer shook his head, making the chain's links grate painfully over his Adam's apple.

"Tell them your name!"

At this moment, Bob knew all was lost. One last act of bravery? A way to end his story heroically? He decided, yes. "Go to Hell."

His captor pulled on the chain again. "Your name!"

Did it matter if he said his name? No. He wasn't a deep-cover officer whose real identity was sacrosanct. As a station chief, he'd been declared to the station's host country. That meant his name was to all intents and purposes public knowledge. "Oakland," he muttered.

"Louder!"

"Bob Oakland!" Saying his name to the camera made him realize something else: he was now a famous spy, retiring with his name on the world's lips. It would have been so good if he could have survived this ordeal because now his story had just gone to a whole new level. His yet-to-be-conceived grandchildren would be in awe.

"Bob Oakland," said the Chechen leader to the camera. "The president of America must decide if Bob Oakland's life is worth anything. If it is not, we will end it. But, I must warn you: we will do so in a manner that will give the world much pause for thought."

As terrible as events were for him, Bob felt a greater fear for Ramzi's fate. The young Jordanian would be made an example of by his fellow-Muslim captors—possibly raped, certainly tortured, and inevitably savaged to the point he would be begging for an end to his life. Oakland's immediate future was now unclear; Ramzi's wasn't. His value to the wannabe-

ISIS recruits was to be killed and thereby warn other Arabs that if they work with infidels, they would be dispatched with comparable unflinching brutality.

Ramzi liked heavy-metal music and spoke in clichés about America. Normally, he had a permanent smile on his face, showing off teeth he polished six times a day. He foolishly tried to charm female soldiers in the way he thought 1940s GIs did when liberating Europe. And he had an annoying habit of wearing fake-crocodile-skin leather loafers that were pointed at the tips and he thought were cool. But that was the worst of Ramzi. Beneath his good-time demeanor and facial hair that alternated between pencil-thin Errol Flynn moustaches and slacker-dude goatees, he was a kid who was destined for university until his medically trained charity-worker parents were kidnapped and executed by Boko Haram terrorists in a Nigerian refugee camp. He'd gone off the rails for a while thereafter. America saved him and gave him renewed purpose.

Until now.

In here, he was nothing but a corpse-in-waiting.

The Chechen leader strode up to the camera, angled his head, and looked into the lens. "In one of your black-site prisons, maybe Guantanamo, you have a young martyr in captivity. We want him released in exchange for Mr. Bob Oakland. Whether you agree to these terms or not, you must post your response on YouTube." The Chechen grinned. "The martyr's name is Arzam Saud."

He switched the video off. Oakland was secured back in place in the corner of the room. The Chechens left the room.

"Ramzi, you okay?"

CHAPTER 4

The president's chief of staff was alone in the White House's subterranean situation room. Men and women who had moments ago sat around the rectangular conference table were now rushing back to their offices in various governme buildings in D.C., all of them in states of high anxiety and u certainty. Donny Tusk didn't share their emotions. Inste he was angry.

Veins were throbbing on the politician's bald head; that were pointed and flush against his cranium, and once earned him the nickname of Vulcan 1 when he w the Green Berets, were red; and the long scar on the s his face—a result of being caught on the wrong side of a line in the First Gulf War—throbbed. He sat staring TV monitor that moments ago had captivated all in th and he didn't look away when Patrick from the CIA

"You wanted to see me," Patrick said as he slum the president's chair at the head of the table.

Tusk pointed toward the screen. "Did you wat Oakland?"

CHAPTER 4

The president's chief of staff was alone in the White House's subterranean situation room. Men and women who had moments ago sat around the rectangular conference table were now rushing back to their offices in various government buildings in D.C., all of them in states of high anxiety and uncertainty. Donny Tusk didn't share their emotions. Instead, he was angry.

Veins were throbbing on the politician's bald head; ears that were pointed and flush against his cranium, and had once earned him the nickname of Vulcan 1 when he was in the Green Berets, were red; and the long scar on the side of his face—a result of being caught on the wrong side of a battle line in the First Gulf War—throbbed. He sat staring at the TV monitor that moments ago had captivated all in the room; and he didn't look away when Patrick from the CIA entered.

"You wanted to see me," Patrick said as he slumped into the president's chair at the head of the table.

Tusk pointed toward the screen. "Did you watch it? Bob Oakland?"

"No, I'm . . ." The Jordanian began weeping. "A traitor to Allah? What will they do to me?"

Bob couldn't answer. He just stared at the poor young man, seeing nothing but misery and despair written across his face. He wondered whether Ramzi had ever truly understood the risks he'd been taking by helping American forces. Perhaps he'd thought he was safer accompanying covert units than taking his chances on the streets. More likely, being in a disastrous situation like this had never occurred to Ramzi.

Ramzi, he decided, had to be protected. Having both of them get out of here alive was all that mattered now. Forget glorious tales to be told on porches to admiring kids. That concept had turned dreadfully sour. "Who's Arzam Saud?"

Ramzi replied, "Never heard of him."

"Me neither." Bob looked above Ramzi's head. "You've got writing behind you on the wall. What does it say?"

Ramzi tried to twist as best he could to view the inscription behind him. In doing so, the chain gripped his throat harder, squeezing on neck muscles and blocking his airway. But the Jordanian persisted until he'd created a sufficient angle to look at the wall and its painted red Arabic letters. He twisted back and slumped, breathing face, his face screwed up in pain.

"It says . . ." Ramzi closed his eyes, raising his face as if to his God. "It says, Dead Room."

"I did."

Tusk rolled up his shirtsleeves, revealing more scars on his muscular forearms. "*Dead Room.* Sons of bitches!"

"What has the president decided?"

"He's listened to those who say we never negotiate with terrorists and therefore can't agree to a trade. And he's listened to others who argue that there needs to be an exception, since Oakland's a high-ranking Agency officer. At the moment, the president's weighing both options." Tusk turned to Patrick. "What are you guys doing?"

Patrick was still. "General Kinnear's mobilized JSOC. The CIA's calling in big-time favors with multiple domestic and foreign agencies. It's a manhunt, and everyone's excited, energetic, working round the clock, totally focused, and determined to find Oakland. And . . ."

"They'll find him dead."

"In all likelihood, yes."

Tusk spun the TV remote on the wooden table. "We're damned every which way we turn."

"Seems that way."

Tusk turned the monitor back on. The image on the screen was the same one frozen after he'd paused the video before the situation room had erupted in a cacophony of indignation thirty minutes ago. Bob Oakland was on his knees, looking smashed up yet defiant, his hands and legs bound in ropes. Six jihadists were standing behind him, one of them gripping a chain that was wrapped around Bob's throat and holding a knife to the CIA officer's gullet. The tethered translator was in the corner of the room, on his ass and looking in even worse shape than Bob. And above them were the red letters.

"It's all over the Internet," muttered Tusk. "We're trying to take the video link down, but the bastards have used multiple sites, and proxy servers, and other shit that I don't understand. No matter what we do, people can find the link if they're looking for it."

Patrick stared at the image. He'd only briefly met Bob Oakland once, and had been struck by the officer's intelligence, charm, and humor. It was also clear that Oakland had tremendous inner strength. But now he was probably praying for a quick death. "Did anyone watching this suggest to the president a neutralizing solution?"

Neutralize all conundrums and persons involved by bombing all suspected ISIS locations; hopefully, strike lucky and kill Oakland and his captors; put Bob out of his misery.

"Yeah, it was mentioned. President's taking it into consideration. It's not a bad option since it means we don't need to negotiate with the scum; nor do we have to fail to recover Oakland alive. And no member of John Q. Public will ever find out that Oakland was more than just an unwitting victim of a surgical strike against ISIS units."

"Tell the president to ignore that option."

"Why?"

"The men holding Oakland and the translator aren't ISIS. Not yet, anyway. And they've told that to the world. These guys won't be using known ISIS facilities. You can't bomb them and claim you were hitting an Islamic State target. Plus..."

"We don't know where they are."

"So you're back to square one."

Tusk rubbed his aching facial scar. "How does it come to

pass that these days a handful of crazies can hold entire states to ransom?" He turned off the T.V. "Who's Arzam Saud?"

"I'm looking in to it. So far I know, he's a full-fledged member of ISIS. We're holding him at Guantanamo."

Tusk stood. "Director Soames tells me you're assigning an asset to investigate how the jihadists knew Oakland, or someone like him, was going to be at the village."

"Correct."

"Who's the asset?"

"I'm not telling you."

"What did you say?!"

"You heard me."

Tusk's anger was palpable. "I've got enough secrets to deal with! Don't need another one!"

Patrick remained calm. "Secrets aren't your biggest problem. Over the coming few days, you're going to have to wade through a heap of unproductive bullshit. You'll have agencies telling you they're making progress—Kinnear advising you that he's putting his men here, there, and everywhere and that his analysts are examining some promising satellite photography; someone presenting new intelligence leads about Oakland's location; and politicians telling you and the president what you should be thinking and doing. Most of it will simply be nothing more than people's justifying their jobs. All of it will most likely prove to be crap."

"You take a pessimistic view of our capabilities."

"You disagree with me?"

The chief of staff was silent.

Patrick continued, "I take a *realistic* view, and I owe it to you to be at least one voice that ain't spouting bullshit. The identity of my asset needs to remain a secret. If I tell you his name, possibly soon someone will force you to appear before a closed-door committee to update them on progress. Maybe you'll have no choice but to reveal the identity of all operators involved. When that happens, egos come into play. I can't afford for my guy to be hindered or compromised because some senators, intelligence officers, or JSOC officers think their limelight's being stolen by someone else." Patrick walked up to Tusk. "*Please*, Donny. No doubt I'm where I am because I don't play politics well, but I've got good instincts. My instincts now tell me that revealing my asset's identity won't help you."

Tusk was deep in thought. "Answer me this: is he good?"

"I wouldn't trust anyone else with this."

It was all Tusk needed to hear. He shook Patrick's hand and returned his attention to the image of Bob Oakland. "You're hoping that if your asset can find out how these guys knew Oakland was going to be at the village, then maybe that information will lead us to his whereabouts. That's beyond a long shot. Increasingly, I'm hoping Bob gets the chance to grab one of the jihadist's guns and turn it on himself."

CHAPTER 5

The following afternoon, a tall gentleman took a seat in the center of the empty stalls in London's Royal Albert Hall. He slung his wet raincoat over the seat next to him, and watched the London Philharmonic Orchestra rehearse Rachmaninoff's Symphony No. 2. Nobody else was in the stalls or the boxes above him. The only reason he was allowed in was because the orchestra's Russian conductor was grateful that six months ago the man had smashed the Russian's cup of tea before the musician could consume its contents of Assam leaves blended with polonium.

The man wore a suit well, and today was no exception; his once-blond hair was now dark, cropped, and greying at the temples; he was muscular though not in an obvious way; his face looked a few years older than his midthirties age because he'd lived a life of hard effort and sorrow; and, depending upon the circumstances, his blue and green eyes alternated between looks of amusement and death. He was handsome to some, less so to others; he carried his frame with a ramrod-straight back, not because he'd once had to do so as a paratrooper on the parade grounds of the French Foreign Legion but rather because he'd been doing so ever since a kindly schoolteacher had told him in his adolescence that his height was nothing to be ashamed of, and he should stop slouching.

His face would be of particular interest to astute observers. Hairless, wrinkled around the eyes, sometimes tanned, other times white, his visage spoke of a loneliness that was superficially content and resigned to its plight. His lips were often angled in a wry smile, one that suggested wisdom, experience, and was a communication to all around him that people should embrace the happiness of life rather than bemoan an existence that had never experienced the horrors he'd seen.

Of course, the same observers would have loved to access the man's mind. But it was a locked vault of terrible memories peppered with recollections of rare moments of joy and imbued with a fearsome cognitive processing power that saw things others couldn't. His brain deliberately eschewed interest in places and inanimate objects in favor of clearing mental space to capture all there was to know about the human condition. Only people interested him.

He was, after all, a spy.

And yet, for all of his insight into the populations of the countries within which he roamed, he often felt detached from those around him, as if he were a human-looking creature who'd fallen to Earth with the instruction to make sense of it all. He hated his detachment and bemusement with the chaos he witnessed and made every effort to blend in as best he could with the people around him. It was as near as he could get to being one of them. To some, he was an Englishman; others, American; he could also convince France, Germany, Russia, and five other nations that he was born and schooled in their countries. It gave him multiple roots though none was as alluring as England. When he wasn't working, he came here because, among other things, he was a journeyman who sometimes liked to return home and listen to Rachmaninov and check that his compatriots were safe and okay.

His eyes were closed as the orchestra embarked on the crescendo of the symphony; his fingers tapping note perfect the armrest of his chair, as if he were the lead violinist; humming the music through his nose with vocal cords that had the ability to range from countertenor to soprano. The tone of his voice reflected this ability. Most people spoke from the front of their mouths. He did so from his lungs, and once the emission reverberated over his cords, it produced a sound that was sometimes as commanding as a general ordering his troops to follow him into battle and others times as sweet and beguiling as a siren calling to those who must trail its notes across misty waters until entrapped and dead.

Of the few people who'd met him and knew his real identity, a handful adored his unwavering compassion, contrarian intellect, and self-sacrifice. They also pitied him.

The majority, however, loathed everything about Will Cochrane.

They wanted him dead.

The Royal Albert Hall is an acoustically flawed venue when at full capacity, but today the sounds emanating from the orchestra soared within the hall's empty cylindrical structure, notes having the space to reach their full potential before finally dying at the back of the stalls and becoming spent as they reached the high dome ceiling. Within the epicenter of the music's full power, Will smiled and kept his eyes shut until the last note was played.

His smile faded as a man took the seat next to him and watched the orchestra start packing up its instruments. "Hello, Patrick."

"How've you been?" asked the CIA director.

"Over what time frame?"

"Recently."

Will kept his eyes on the stage. "Of late I've been listening to a rehearsal of a score composed by a dead Moldovan whose genius outshone the faux-aristocratic bent of his snobbish and impoverished family. The orchestra's 96 percent there. The upper strings need to pay attention to their tempo in the second movement's ostinato; and the solo clarinetist and oboe section might wish to consider increasing their volume in the third movement, to compensate for this building's acoustics. But otherwise I'm satisfied the ensemble will be ready for the performance tomorrow evening."

"I meant, what has your employer been doing with you?"

"My employer . . ."

The Secret Intelligence Service, otherwise known as MI6.

" . . . has moved on to other matters. It believes our little *project* has run its course."

The project he was referring to was Task Force S—the joint CIA-MI6 unit to which Will had belonged and been its lead field agent. Alongside Will's MI6 controller, Patrick had been co-head of the force until it had been disbanded at the behest of powerful individuals on both sides of the Atlantic who were envious of its success.

Will looked at Patrick. "Recently, I've been signing bits of paper telling me to keep my mouth shut because I'm persona non grata and in a few months will officially be a *former* intelligence officer."

Out of MI6. No job. No more excuse for him to skulk in the recesses of the secret world because he's paid to do so by Her Majesty's government.

Will added, "I imagine you're not in a dissimilar position."

Patrick felt exposed in the cavernous building and wondered how a man with Will's covert profile felt so comfortable being here. "Pretty much, except I'm still in a job for the foreseeable future. I guess the Agency's put me into the *keep-your-enemies-closer* category."

Will watched the last person leave the stage. It was the conductor; a man who'd once been a Russian SVR asset turned MI6 double agent. No doubt he was worried about tomorrow night's performance. Forever in his life, he would be dreading the day a man like Will Cochrane wasn't by his side to rescue him from an inevitable further Russian attempt on his life.

"I'm bored," said Will. "I'm hoping you're not, and that's why you wanted to see me."

"Bored?"

"Fractious. Prone to impulsive and illogical decisions based on the sole desire to wrong-foot myself and everyone I know." Will stared at Patrick; right now, his eyes were dead. "Bob Oakland's plight worries you, yes?"

"You guessed that's why I'm here."

"I never guess. When did you leave D.C. for Britain?"

"Late East Coast time this morning."

"Your wife made you breakfast before you left?"

"Actually, I made *her* our breakfast."

"I'm sorry."

"Because she didn't fix me food? She's a working woman and has every right not to play housewife."

"No. I'm sorry because I've now established that your wife was with you at breakfast. She's an interior designer with a gift for attention to detail. Plus, she's borderline OCD. It wouldn't have escaped her attention over breakfast that her husband had missed a bit of stubble when shaving. Either she let you leave the house looking like that because she no longer cares about your relationship, or she's upset with you. It's the latter. You need to let her install the ceiling-height windows she wants in your house."

"How in God's name did you know about the windows?" Patrick was flustered. "And you've only met my wife once!"

"She's curious about the world. All she wants is to look at things. Windows allow that. Give her what she wants, and everything will be good. It will be a kind gesture."

"It will make our home look like a giant greenhouse!"

"A kind gesture," Will repeated. "She adores you. Make her happy."

Patrick nodded. "Hadn't thought of it that way." He needed to change the conversation. "Sounds like you've got some spare time on your hands. Fancy a freelance job?"

"To find Bob Oakland and his translator?" Will interlocked his scarred hands. "The intelligence and special-operations communities of the United States will have that task in hand."

"The task, maybe, but not the likelihood of a result. It's . . ."

"Thousands of square miles to cover in northern Iraq and western Syria. Needle-in-a-haystack territory. And I'll add no value by getting on a plane to the Middle East to join the queue of others pursuing that fool's quest."

Patrick had expected this response. "I'm not asking you to do that. I've got full authority from Capitol Hill to look at this from whatever perspective I choose; more accurately, from the perspective of whichever asset I choose. I'm hoping you'll say yes." Patrick withdrew a copy of today's *Washington Post*. On its front cover was a photo of Oakland in the dead room.

"We want you to establish how Oakland and his team were compromised at the village. Somebody who knew they were going to be there has either got loose lips or is on the payroll of some nasties. Find that person, and you might find a more productive path to the jihadists holding Oakland and the translator."

Will took the paper and stared at the shot of Bob Oakland. Before seeing him earlier in the day in an edited newschannel broadcast of the jihadists' video, Will had never set eyes on the man or heard of him. Nor had the news channel been permitted to reveal any information about Oakland beyond confirming the he was an American citizen and a government employee. "Married with grown-up children, I suspect."

"Yes."

"A senior officer, and highly regarded by his peers. But, he's not a backstabbing careerist. He's achieved his rank by selfless service and merit. His eyes suggest a smart man; wisdom's in them, also a trace of humor."

"That about sums him up."

"A year, maybe much less, to retirement."

"He had a few weeks until he was out. The man should've been coasting to retirement."

"But he didn't because he deserved a story."

"What?"

Will placed a finger against the photo. "He spent his career putting himself second; did whatever was needed; went places others turned their noses up at because there was no glory to be had there. Bob has been a through-and-through professional. But, facing retirement, all he asked of the Agency was one thing in return for his lifelong duty. He remembered his childhood; one spent reading tales of adventure and daring. Before he walked off into the sunset, he wanted the Agency to give him a piece of the action."

Patrick laughed. "You can't know that for sure."

"I can't. But I posit the notion because it's better than having no notion at all. Plus, I'm right." Will handed the paper back to his former boss. "He's lost in his adventure, and no one can find him."

"And that's why I need you to find who sold him out. The president's chief of staff and the head of the Agency agree."

"Their idea's wrong."

Patrick sighed. "Why doesn't it surprise me to hear you say that?"

Will placed the tips of his fingers against his nose. "The search to find Oakland and a security leak are futile because both will take too long. We must turn our thinking on its head and construct another starting point."

"That's fine as long as you've got an idea where it will lead."

"I've several hypotheses as to where it could lead, and one in particular fascinates me. But ideas are useless without supporting data. In the video, the jihadists stated they wanted a man called Arzam Saud in exchange for Oakland. Who is Saud?"

Patrick told him what little he knew.

"Our starting point is for you to travel back to the States and find out everything you can about your ISIS prisoner. Don't assume what I need to know. Find out *everything*. Then, relay what you know to me."

"Why's that your starting point?"

Will didn't answer.

CHAPTER 6

On the outskirts of the Renaissance-era city of Lucca in Tuscany, the Russian oligarch and property tycoon Viktor Gorsky smiled as he watched the sun mellow into a blood-red haze while it descended over the horizon. It was, as he'd hoped, at the time of day when his newlywed daughter was scheduled to have her first dance with her husband in front of the hundreds of guests in the grounds of his mansion.

Throughout all of yesterday and today, Gorsky had been a bag of nerves: fretting about the wisdom or otherwise of having the wedding and its aftermath celebrations alfresco; worrying that the flower displays would wilt in the heat; checking over and over again the settings on the starched white cloths that covered the dining tables within his orchard; feeling his blood pressure rise as the female wedding coordinator would break off from yelling orders at the legions of wedding staff to tell him for the tenth time in as many minutes that she was fairly certain everything was going according to plan; and phoning and rephoning vintners, caterers, the string quartet, the priest, the jazz band, the supplier of white

doves that were to be launched in the air after his daughter had tied the knot, and the baker who seemed reasonably confident his cake wouldn't melt when it was displayed.

Had his daughter gotten married a few years earlier, Gorsky's wife would have willingly absorbed the stress of the wedding, allowing her husband to sit back and sip too many glasses of Cinzano while he watched preparations. But his wife had passed away last year. He'd had to step up to the plate and ensure his only child got the sendoff she deserved.

Now, the jazz band was playing. His daughter looked considerably more relaxed than she'd been earlier in the day, tossing her auburn hair back onto her flowing white dress as she laughed, embracing her husband, and allowing him to spin her as the guests quaffed champagne and whooped and cheered. All was good. The evening was warm but not oppressive; lanterns suspended from apple and orange trees were being lit; his twenty acres of land were as enchanting as a fairy tale, yet its lawns were manicured and its stone paths designed to perfection, a good thing since half of the guests were in high heels. People were well fed. The cake hadn't melted. The best man's speech had been polite. And the usually voracious appetite of the Martelli family seemed to be showing signs of restraint, given the family was not yet any drunker than the forty other clans in attendance.

The evening would be a long one, and Gorsky could now relax. He clapped his hands in time to the music as his daughter spun faster, her laugh pleasing him as much as it had when she was three years old and would run to him when he returned home after work.

"Papa, Papa!" she'd exclaim while launching her tiny body

into his arms, throwing her head back and giggling with glee as if the daily moment had never happened before and was one of pure ecstasy.

Gorsky hadn't changed since then. But his daughter was now grown-up, and here he was giving her away. He hoped she'd visit often from her new home in Umbria even though he'd told her not to worry about her papa and that she must now live her new life. He gulped his aperitif in an effort to suppress a tear.

"Mr. Gorsky," said one of his many bodyguards as he approached his boss. "You have a telephone call. Urgent."

Gorsky snapped, "I told you—no telephone calls yesterday or today unless they're to do with my daughter's wedding."

"Urgent," the burly guard repeated while looking a little uneasy. "It's from one of your associates."

Gorsky slammed his glass down on the drinks table by his side, fixed a grin on his face, and walked between tables and chairs containing relatives, acquaintances, friends of the bride and groom, businessmen and -women, and trained killers.

"Signor Gorsky," many of them said as he passed them and shook their hands, "today you must be so proud."

He walked into his huge and tasteful mansion, entered his study, and picked up the telephone. "Yes?" He listened to the caller for one minute, before saying, "Make sure nothing comes back to me. They'll find out we did business together, and that's fine. But that's all they must know."

Bob Oakland had no idea whether it was day or night when the three jihadists entered the windowless chamber, removed the chain from his throat, and dragged him out of the room; its walls echoing the hysterical cries of Ramzi who remained tethered in the dead room.

Oakland's head pounded against the stone floor, his lips were cracked and ragged, and one of his eyes was shut because of a punch. He was hauled into a smaller room. It contained a black hangman's rope fixed on the ceiling and below it a wooden bench the size of a mortuary slab.

His captors breathed fast as they lifted Oakland onto the bench and put his head in the noose. The tallest of the Chechens was the man who'd previously dictated his terms to the president of the United States while holding Oakland on a leash and pressing a knife against his throat. He stood in front of Oakland while his colleagues kept hold of the CIA officer's arms.

"You wish for a quick death?"

Oakland lowered his head; his brain felt like a powerful hand was squeezing it to pulp. "Do I have a choice?"

"You are"—the Chechen frowned as if trying to establish what he was going to say next—"a puppet on a string, are you not?"

That's exactly what Oakland felt like.

"What will you say?"

Oakland frowned. "Say?"

"Final words. A dead man must have his final words."

Bob wanted to spit in the man's face. It would've served no purpose. "Please tell my wife and daughters that I'm sorry."

The Chechen leader took a step closer to the bench and Oakland. "Go out of this world with dignity, not regret! I won't give you a quick death unless your final words deserve it."

Bob smiled. Better final words? He recalled his trek in the desert, a walk wholly unlike that of T. E. Lawrence in magnitude but not in spirit. At least, not according to the David Lean movie depiction of the Englishman. A line from the movie stuck in his head.

"My final sentence is as follows." Oakland spoke the words uttered by the actor who'd played Lawrence in the film. "The truth is, I'm an ordinary man."

"I doubt that." The jihadist nodded at his men, who swept Oakland's legs off the bench.

He dropped to his death, a split second left of life, with Oakland hoping his body weight would cause his neck to snap when the rope became taut. Or maybe it wouldn't, and he'd be allowed several seconds more of life to recall other memories while his legs thrashed.

He crashed to the ground, the rope still around his neck but its length no longer fixed to anything firm.

A mock execution.

His captors laughed.

The Chechen leader stamped on Oakland's head and held it flush against the floor. "It's not that simple. If Arzam Saud is given to us, you'll walk out of here alive. If the American president decides that you must die, we'll hang you for real."

Oakland was hauled back into the dead room and chained against the wall. Thirty feet away, in the opposite corner, Ramzi wept. "What happened, Mr. Oakland?"

Bob told him.

"Will your country agree to the jihadists' demands?"

Bob thought it unlikely though he didn't know. He felt the chain tighten around his throat as he leaned forward. "No matter what they say, they're not going to give us a quick death. It will take mental strength to do this, but if we can get to our knees and lean forward, we might be able to get the chains to strangle us."

Both men tried. And both men failed; their instincts to survive kicking in quickly and forcing their bodies to adopt an alleviating position that caused the chains to slacken. Ramzi used his bound hands to strike his forehead with frustration. Oakland just sat, blinking fast as he stared at the solitary ceiling bulb in the center of the room.

"They must rescue us," cried out Ramzi.

Oakland shook his head. "It took us ten years to find someone as recognizable as bin Laden. How long do you think it will take them to find a Jordanian kid and a guy from Montana?"

Ramzi prodded the ground, his usual good looks and enthusiastic demeanor cast aside in favor of actions that seemed to belong to an aging ape that had strayed too far from his patch and been caught unawares by other predators or the climate. He was touching the land, willingly preparing for death.

Oakland wanted his mind to grow wings and leave his doomed body. "They say I can be free. They make no mention of you."

"I know," said the Arab. "I wanted a different life."

"Me too. At least, a different ending to the life I've led." Quietly, Oakland added, "We just have each other now."

CHAPTER 8

Ninety-three miles southwest of Washington, D.C., is an old redbrick mansion that had in its history been the location of a murder, a suicide, a training ground for World War II OSS agents, an institute for the insane, and a beatnik poets' retreat until they'd been evicted from the premises after a hallucinogenic-fueled weeklong orgy of free love had culminated in the crazed poets spilling naked into the neighboring village.

The government had repossessed the home and its grounds and totally renovated the property, returning it to the sumptuous glory favored by its first owner—a nineteenth-century high-court judge who'd by day practiced law in D.C. and by night had dined on flesh whose consumption was banned. During the last few decades it had been a discreet place for senior spies to gather and discuss matters of national importance, for high-ranking defectors to be housed, debriefed, and entertained, and for security-cleared senators to be taught the ways of the secret world and how to move within it while keeping one's mouth shut.

Today it was devoid of all such characters though it was brimming with personnel whose sole area of expertise was ensuring that people could never escape their grasp.

Patrick showed his pass to the armed guardsmen at the razor-wire perimeter, waited while they checked the inside and underside of his vehicle for bombs or anything else untoward, and drove his vehicle onward along the sweeping gravel driveway before bringing his car to a halt in front of the huge house.

Before the CIA officer could get out of the car, a young man in a suit was by the driver's window. He tapped on the glass. "ID."

"I've already shown it at the gate."

"ID," the official repeated with the charisma of an airport immigration officer at the end of a hectic shift.

Patrick held his passport to the window. "This do?"

"You don't have Agency identification?"

"Nobody does," replied Patrick, making no attempt to hide his impatience. "But you should be expecting me, plus I'm carrying the letter of introduction you needed."

"Come with me."

Patrick exited his car and followed the man into the house. He'd been there before, and though many things had remained the same—the oak-paneled walls, gilt-framed paintings, lavish furnishings, and other trappings of a government department that has an unaccountable budget—some things were very different. There was a body scanner in the entrance, numerous armor-clad penitentiary officers, and walls of iron bars that had been fixed in place from ceilings to floors. The people who'd taken over the building had transformed it into a high-security prison.

After Patrick emptied his pockets, removed his belt from around his suit pants, and walked through the scanner with his arms held apart, a middle-aged man appeared on the other side of the bars. "You the CIA guy?"

Patrick nodded, wishing the man hadn't shouted out his vocation so loudly.

"Give me the letter." The man held his hand between the bars, expectant.

"Are you in charge?" asked Patrick as he handed the man a sheet that contained the seal of the Agency and its director's signature.

"Temporarily while my men are *temporarily* here. You wouldn't believe what we had to do to make this property fit for our purpose. There are so many better places we could have transferred the prisoner to. God knows why we were told to come here."

"It's secret." Patrick moved into a cage, its door behind him locked back into place while another was opened so he could proceed into the inner perimeter of the newly constructed fortress. "Your name?"

"Henry Kane." The prison governor was a plump man, with receding hair and glasses that were balanced on the tip of his nose. "I was in the special wing at Guantanamo before you guys thought me and my boys might like a whiff of Virginia air. Damn inconvenience."

"Where are you keeping him?"

"In the living room. It was the only place big enough to house our cell. We need to see him from all angles." Kane frowned. "The prisoner wasn't in the special wing at The Bay, because he's just some lowlife. He's a terrorist alright but a *nobody* terrorist. Now, we've moved him here, and we're treating him like Public Enemy Number One. We've given him the Hannibal Lector treatment. He doesn't deserve it."

"It's not who he is that matters; the reason he's here is because of who wants him." Patrick imagined Will Cochrane telling him he was probably only partially right on that observation. "I need to see him alone."

Kane looked affronted. "The guards will have to stay."

"Your guards can grab a coffee. Read the letter."

Kane did so, his expression angry. "Jeez. You bunch of amateurs."

"And the file in your hands. I want it."

The file on the prisoner.

Kane threw the file at Patrick, pointed at the entrance to the living room, and walked in. Inside resembled a gentleman's club. But the interior's fittings had been rearranged. Rouge sofas that had many times been used by cigar-smoking men of many nationalities, talking to each other in hushed tones, sometimes sitting in silence while looking out of windows at the grounds, had been pushed to the walls. A billiards table was upended and flush against bay windows; once it had had pride of place in the center of the room. Patrick recalled playing a frame on it with a gravel-voiced senior MI6 officer who'd potted a black before dusting the tip of his cue, looking at Patrick, and proclaiming, "Double agent Gregor is slipperier than a spunked-over billiard ball." Mahogany side tables that were usually dotted around the room so coffees or tumblers of whiskey could be rested on them were stacked in a pile. Rails supporting heavy velvet curtains now had the additional burden of surveillance cameras. Only the wall-mounted library and huge paintings depicting scenes from the War of Independence and Civil War remained in their usual place. Ordinarily, the room was eye-catching and exuded a powerful ambience of being a top secret retreat from the overt and covert worlds. Indeed, the whole mansion carried the nickname Purgatory because spies who came here thought it was a place in limbo. Today, everything paled into insignificance compared to the huge steel cage that was in middle of the room. Inside it were a bed, a table and chair, a portable latrine, a pile of books, and a dark-skinned, thin young man who would have been handsome were it not for the long, unkempt beard that made him look like a mad monk.

Arzam Saud. The ISIS terrorist jihadists wanted in exchange for Bob Oakland.

He was standing by one side of his prison, wearing an orange jumpsuit, his feet bare, his hands gripping the bars, while he watched Patrick.

Four guards were outside the cage, on each corner of the asymmetrical cubicle. Reluctantly, Kane told them to leave.

"And you," said Patrick to the governor.

"God damn it!"

"Please. Go."

As Kane walked out while muttering threats about making official complaints, Patrick grabbed a wooden chair and sat opposite the young ISIS member, only bars separating them. He said nothing for five minutes, just stared at the prisoner, with his legs folded and his hands clasped. "You speak English?"

"Is that a statement or a question? The intonation in your voice suggests the latter though your absence of a proper sentence construct instructs me that *I* speak better English than you do." Saud's accent was barely noticeable.

Patrick smiled while flicking through the file. "Schooled in England. Wealthy Bahraini parents. They allowed you to access some of their wealth. You used it in business. Then you joined ISIS."

"I've lived a rich life."

"You're only twenty-three."

"Then I'm doubly blessed to have so much good fortune squeezed within so few years. I must be the envy of many." Saud sat on the floor, his legs crossed in the lotus position, his hands resting on his lap.

"You know why you're here? Who I am? Why I'm here?"

"Three questions in rapid succession. How can you value the answers to those questions if you toss them all at once at me? Surely, you'd prefer to give me each question piecemeal in the hope of fuller and more instructive answers. Instead, you strike me as a pathetic blue-collar gambling addict who's throwing all his dimes into different slot machines, hoping one of them will pay out."

Patrick didn't respond.

Saud shook his head, an expression of contempt on his face. "I'm not afforded the luxury of a television, access to the Internet and newspapers, and nor do I have friends and family visiting me and telling me what's happening in the outside world. I'm not clairvoyant. It would be impossible for me to know why I'm here and why you're here. But, as to who you are, I would imagine you're CIA, NSA, or FBI."

"Why do you think that?"

"That's better—one question at a time." Saud's expression

softened. "It's a case of *interested parties*. Who's interested in
me? Of course, people who are interested in the ranks of ISIS.
That would include special divisions of the United States military, but you don't belong there." Saud frowned. "Actually, a
long time ago you might have been in the military, I'd guess."

"You're sure?"

Saud looked exasperated when he replied, "A guess ne-
gates certainty. But you have the deportment of a military
man, and your cheap clothes have been cared for by you in
the way a man who's spent a bit of time in the military can't
break the habit of ensuring he never leaves the house without
pants that are immaculately pressed. A further guess would
be army, possibly infantry." He held up his hand in case Patrick was going to interject. "But once again, it's a guess."

"You have an eye for detail."

"When you spend all day in places like these, it's easy to
notice the little things." Saud lowered his hand. "Something
that isn't a guess is a deduction about your expression. It suggests lack of conventional thinking. Blindly following orders
in the army was a long time ago. Since then, you've been allowed to break rules. I suggest that means we can drop the
possibility of the FBI. That leaves NSA or CIA. But you don't
look like a computer number cruncher to me. So, I'm betting
you're CIA."

Patrick held his stare.

"Strange, though, that the CIA would employ an illiter-
ate man who doesn't know how to interrogate people." Saud
grinned, showing off immaculate white teeth.

Patrick closed the file and smoothed a hand over its cover.
"You're here because a bunch of crazies want us to release

you in exchange for an American hostage. Why do you think you're of value to them?"

"I've no idea."

"Nor do I, and that's the problem."

"Why?"

"Because if I knew why they wanted you, I could make an informed decision whether to keep you locked up or not."

Saud's grin remained. "I'm sorry I couldn't be of more help. Perhaps if you'd improved your interrogation technique, things might have been different."

Patrick was very still when he responded, "I didn't come here to interrogate you. I came here to *look* at you. And what I see is a dumb kid who thinks a good education has made him smart when in fact it's just given a rich brat a few words. Mom and Dad had to give you their money so you could play at being successful. And when that didn't work out, you thought you'd play at being a fundamentalist. Thing is, though, you sucked at that as well. Got yourself caught in Iraq. In prison. In here. Just some dumb kid who's looking at me through bars."

Saud's smile vanished.

Patrick stood. "The president isn't going to cut a deal with ISIS over some loser like you. And that means you're going to rot in here until you die."

To Patrick's surprise, Arzam Saud burst out laughing.

CHAPTER 9

Simpson's in the Strand was usually Will Cochrane's favorite London restaurant at lunchtime. It unashamedly harked back to bygone Victorian and Edwardian sensibilities about how one should fuel one's mind and body. Chess masters once practiced their craft here; authors including E. M. Forster, P. G. Wodehouse, and Sir Arthur Conan Doyle, dined in the venue and used it as a location in their works of literature; and everyone who came here did so because it was one of the last bastions of a traditional English roast dinner. Today was not much different from how Will imagined the restaurant had been throughout its near-two-century existence. For sure, outside, noisy cars jammed the bustling Strand wherein once there would have been the soporific sounds of horses' hooves tapping the road as the beasts pulled carriages. But inside, time had stood still. Then and now, deferential waiters in starched white shirts and black uniforms pushed huge trolleys containing roasted lumps of cow and pig toward expectant diners, and the waiters were wearing looks of pride and appreciation while they brandished razor-sharp knives and asked customers if they could be tempted by some slices of the meat. The majority of the restaurant was taken up by exposed tables that were positioned a respectful distance from each other, but along one wall oak booths were available for individuals who cherished their privacy. Simpson's was an establishment that catered to those who wished to be seen and those who didn't.

Will was sitting alone in one of the booths.

Though he found them in equal measure amusing and endearing, it wasn't the pomp, ceremony, and cuisine that drew Will to Simpson's. It was the people who came here. Today was no different from other days, and Will should have drawn wonder from the people he could see—a three-star general dining alone in full parade uniform and washing his meal down with a bottle of Pouilly-Fumé, a stoic expression on his face suggesting he was partaking of his last meal before battle; a bishop and rabbi gesticulating madly at each other over their plates of calves liver and lamb rump before laughing in unison as if they suddenly realized the absurdity of their conflicting passions; a well-known female Member of Parliament blushing and slapping her good-looking young male political aide; and a party of high-ranking civil-service mandarins—all men, all wearing pin-striped suits, and all with eyebrows the size of combs—speaking to each other in grunts, carefully crafted haughty looks of disdain on their jowly faces. But Will's mind was elsewhere as he halfheartedly picked at his meal of venison. He thought only of Bob Oakland and his Jordanian translator, shackled in a stifling hot room, no food, no liquid of any kind to satiate their parched bodies.

Patrick sat opposite him, grabbed the menu, and tossed it back down.

"Don't you want to eat?" Will's voice sounded as distant as the thoughts in his mind.

"Damn airplane food's given me the shits."

"Delightful."

"Not for me, it ain't." Patrick's irritability was as palpable as the fatigue etched on his face. "I was downgraded to economy. Mother and kid were next to me. Kid was screaming the whole flight. I bought him toys from Duty Free, plus a cool kid's watch that I thought would distract him. I think the poor boy's ears were suffering from cabin pressure."

"Encouraging him to yawn would have helped."

"Next time, I'll keep that in mind." The CIA officer glanced around. "Why do you insist on meeting me in public? We could've met at your home."

Will shrugged. "You're still a spook. I'm not, and that means I need witnesses when I meet with you. Plus, I'm refurbishing my home. It's a mess."

"Witnesses?" Patrick laughed. "Nobody notices you. Or me for that matter."

"Isn't that the point? Nobody notices us. Such a shame." Will pushed his plate away, deciding he'd feign lack of appetite and apologize to the waiter. "What have you got for me?"

Patrick told Will about his encounter with Arzam Saud, his impressions of the young man, and the scant data on him within the prison file. "He joined ISIS eight months ago and was captured by pro-US Yazidis in northern Iraq two months ago. He's believed to be a foot soldier in ISIS and carries no rank owing to his junior status."

Will frowned. "His profile's wrong for a prisoner exchange. There are hundreds of men and women in US captivity who'd make far more important exchanges—al Qaeda commanders, Taliban leaders, a whole bunch of high-profile lunatics. Why aren't the ISIS wannabes asking for the release of one of them?"

Patrick replied, "Saud's got money. Inherited. Probably oil cash. I reckon they want him sprung so he can help fund ISIS."

"Any details about what he did with his money before he joined ISIS?"

"Mostly property deals in Europe." Patrick looked around again to ensure he wasn't being overheard. "The biggest ones were in partnership with Russian billionaire Viktor Gorsky. Gorsky's a private man, very little known about him. He's a recluse. But, there's one guy who knows more about Gorsky than most. Investigative journalist called Eddie Lanes. Works for the British newspaper *The Independent*. Trouble is, he's in hiding after receiving death threats."

"Death threats from Gorsky or people employed by him?"

"Could be. Or maybe they're from someone else Lanes has investigated. Either way, there's no proof."

Will was deep in thought. "I need to find out about Gorsky."

Patrick slammed his hand on the table. "We're running out of time! Most likely Saud and Gorsky have no relevance to helping us find Oakland."

"Most likely." Quietly, Will added, "But Saud's profile is all wrong. The British police will know where Lanes is. Pull some strings, so I can meet with him."

CHAPTER 10

The great and the powerful filed into the White House's subterranean situation room. Sight of the politicians made chief of staff Donny Tusk feel like an exasperated school-teacher who was witnessing his Ivy-League-destined charges saunter into class late, all of the pupils with egos the size of small planets. The president had told Tusk many times that the reason he was chief of staff was because he understood public service and had no aspirations for the top job in politics. This was true, and it made the president trust his loyal aide. And it made Tusk despise the Machiavellian agendas of the men and women he had to marshal at meetings like these. It was like trying to herd cats, he often thought, all of them preening themselves, wishing to be the center of attention, and going in whatever direction they damn well liked.

The president was sitting next to him; Tusk could sense his unease.

When all were seated and had exhausted their greetings to one another and fake pleasantries, Tusk banged his fist three times on the rectangular table as if he were a judge with a gavel. "Let's get this over with."

The room was silent; all faced the television monitor on the wall. Donny Tusk turned on the TV and prepared to press Play on the video that had been sent to him an hour ago by NSA technicians who'd been looking out for it on the Web. Probably, some in the room had already seen the video, hopping onto YouTube or similar with their insecure smartphones or other gadgets that Tusk had no care to understand. Nevertheless, all were expectant. It was a rare moment in the situation room when you could hear a pin drop.

Tusk pressed Play.

The image of the dead room was blurred at first, but then someone behind the camera brought the lens into focus. Bob Oakland was on his knees; his face was a swollen pulp, his shirt was ripped and smeared in blood, and his hair was lank and plastered to his scalp. Behind him were two men, one tall, the other shorter yet with a broad physique. They were two of the men who'd appeared in the first video Tusk had seen of Oakland. The taller was holding Oakland on a chain leash that was wrapped around the CIA officer's throat. In the corner of the room, the Jordanian translator Ramzi was chained to the wall. Ropes around his legs, torso, and arms, would have made it impossible for him to move though they looked unnecessary right now because Ramzi's head was slumped onto his chest. He was either unconscious or dead. And behind Ramzi were the red Arabic letters.

Dead Room.

One of the female senators in the room held her hand to

her mouth and exclaimed, "Dear God. What have they done to them?"

"Quiet," said Tusk. He shared the politician's concern, but now all in the room had to stay focused.

The shorter jihadist thrust a single sheet of paper into Oakland's hands, said in accented English, "Read," and held a knife to the American's throat.

Oakland raised his head and looked into the camera. The man operating the camera zoomed in so that Oakland's head took up most of the screen. It was impossible to tell whether he looked in agony or resigned to a terrible death. Punches and kicks to the face, and hands gripping his matted hair and pummeling his skull against the concrete floor, had earlier distorted all normal expressions beyond recognition. It pained Tusk when the involuntary thought entered his head that Oakland now looked like a seal pup that had been clubbed to death.

The CIA officer tried to speak, but his voice croaked. He darted a look at his captors. Hoarsely, he managed to utter, "Water, please. Water."

There was laughter, the sound of footsteps walking quickly out of the room, and upon their return Oakland's face was still taking up most of the screen when from one side of him a bucket of water was emptied over his face.

More laughter from the jihadists.

Oakland moaned and lowered his head.

The chain around his throat was yanked back, allowing all watching the video to see the man's bashed and sodden visage. It took all of Tusk's restraint not to punch the table. Oakland coughed, blinked fast and looked at the sheet. "I must read this?"

"You must," said the tall jihadist.

Oakland read what was on the paper. "In four days I will be dead. In less than four days, the man who shares my room will be dead. Nothing has changed. We are experiments, my . . . *friends* assure me. Experiments to ascertain the true strength and resilience of the human body. If you don't cooperate, it is inevitable that we will become cadavers. What is less certain is how long it will take." Bob looked straight into the camera. "Don't give in to these bastards."

"Only say what's on the paper!" barked one of the jihadists.

"Fuck you!"

One of the jihadists moved to Ramzi and put the tip of his knife against the translator's eyeball. "Finish reading what's on the paper!"

There was no doubting now that resignation was in Oakland's expression as he finished articulating the script. "Mr. President: it is within your power to release an American, a man, a husband, a father, a loyal servant of the United States. I am that man. Arzam Saud is of no use to you. Just let him go. If you do not, you will be telling the rest of American society that you would do the same to them."

Oakland dropped the paper while murmuring, "Bastards."

A fist punched his head to one side.

The video ended.

There was silence in the White House room for several seconds before the place erupted with noise from its occupants. Indignation was rife. People were shouting. Only the president and Tusk remained still and silent.

A heated debate ensued, some arguing that there was nothing that could be done aside from continuing the search for the CIA officer and others saying that Saud was just a junior ISIS pawn, and his release wouldn't damage national security. The president pondered the debate. When the room was silent, he said, "There is another option. Saud is suspected of being involved in a car bombing in Jordan. We transfer him to Jordan to allow them to do what they want with him. The Jordanians are more open to considering negotiating with terrorists. And one of the prisoners is Jordanian. Let Jordan do the prisoner exchange. That way, we get our guy back but don't lose face."

More opinions and anger were hurled across the room, not necessarily directed at anyone in particular; rather, the room's occupants were brimming with emotions they couldn't control but just had to release. Tusk knew now that his analogy of being a schoolmaster amid gifted children was correct. He was Robin Williams, locking horns with Matt Damon in the movie *Good Will Hunting*. Damon was trying to outsmart Williams with his knowledge of art, literature, architecture, and travel. But Damon had never flown on a plane let alone left the country. Damon thought his mind could supplant the five senses of smell, touch, hearing, taste, and sight. He was wrong and had no further retorts when Williams told him he was just a kid who couldn't understand the Sistine Chapel just because he'd read about it. He had to be there, expose his senses to it in person. That's how Tusk felt now. He'd smelled his friends' dead bodies rot on battlefields. His finger had curled around his trigger when young Iraqi men who should never have been in conflict charged toward him brandishing their guns. He'd heard the whistle of mortars and lost his hearing when they exploded. Had given mouth-to-mouth resuscitation to friends and foe. And he'd climbed mountains to see and fight men whose loyalty was to the earth, not humanity. They were the worst: the ones who were like tigers in the back of caves. But the people in this room were Matt Damon—gifted, ticking the box of experience by imagining what it looked like.

They told the president he was wrong. Regrettably, the president listened to them.

CHAPTER 11

The ferry berthed in the small town of Stornoway in the Isle of Lewis, Outer Hebrides. Because of high winds out at sea, the journey from the Scottish mainland had taken twenty minutes longer than its scheduled time of two hours and forty-five minutes, but that didn't bother the captain of the vessel because the ferry only ran twice a day. He had plenty of time to restock the ship before making the return journey.

The wind had abated though a heavy rain persisted and prompted disembarking foot passengers to open umbrellas and run. One man in a suit and overcoat seemed unconcerned by the weather. He walked slowly toward a police car, outside of which was a young Scottish constable whose face was screwed up as if it were being pelted by battery acid.

Will Cochrane showed him fake ID. "Toby Groves. Am I in the right place?"

The police officer shielded his eyes as he glanced at Will's passport and nodded. "Aye, if you like rain." He opened the passenger door. "Get in."

They drove along a coastline containing fishing vessels

and yachts, and through the pretty seaside town, before heading west over rugged countryside. Will had never been to the Outer Hebrides before though he knew they were a good place for a man to lie low. A long string of interconnected islands that ran beyond the entire northwestern seaboard of mainland Scotland, the Hebrides were sparsely populated with people who made it their business to know who entered their shores. The communities here were tight-knit and suspicious of strangers until they could prove they meant dwellers or their stunning lands no harm.

"Are you from here?" Will asked the constable.

The officer increased the speed of his windshield wipers to compensate for the rain. "No. I was transferred from Ullapool a year ago. What's London like?"

"You've never been?"

"No, and I've no reason to."

"It's full of murderers. You'd have your work cut out if you were transferred there."

"Not for me, thank you. The worst we get up here are land disputes and people knowing too much about each other. That suits me fine." He glanced at Will. "MI5's like the FBI, right?"

In conjunction with the Metropolitan Police's Special Branch, Patrick had arranged for Will to pose as a member of Britain's Security Service, MI5.

"It's a bit like that except we don't have powers of arrest. We need the police for that."

"But not today?"

"I just need you to make introductions and vouch for my credentials."

They drove for a further thirty minutes, on narrow roads through flat heathland that contained no signs of human life, before reaching the western coast, where the scenery was mountainous, windswept, and looked inhospitable in the lashing rain.

"There we are," said the police officer while pointing at his windshield.

Ahead of them was an isolated house, sitting atop a cliff. On either side of it was nothing but countryside, a few sheep that were huddled in groups, and the escarpments of two mountains. The constable stopped his car outside the house, pressed his horn, and got out. Will followed him.

A man emerged from the house. He was in his early forties, overweight, wearing jeans and an oilskin jacket with its hood up, and had one hand cupped over a cigarette in his mouth.

"How's it going?" asked the young police officer while smiling.

The man looked angry. "Just fine," he replied with a gruff London accent.

"Any problems since I was last here?"

"Just bloody sheep trashing my garden. Can't you tell Hamish to get them away from here?"

The constable laughed. "It's his farm's grazing rights. You know that." He pointed at Will. "This is the fellow I told you about. The one from London."

The man pulled his hood down. His chubby face was stubbly and his brown hair ruffled. "I said I didn't want to be disturbed."

The constable shrugged. "And I said you won't be disturbed by anyone apart from the police. Mr. Groves is sort of police. That means he can see you."

"*Sort of* police?" The man flicked his cigarette away.

Will said, "I'm from Thames House." It was a reference to the headquarters of MI5.

"Ah." The man's hostility appeared to increase. "You're a *stay-at-home* spy."

Will asked, "Can I come in?"

"Do I have a choice?"

"No." Will glanced at the police officer. "You'll wait for me out here?"

The officer nodded and got back into his car, grateful to be out of the inclement weather.

Will followed the man into his home. He immediately knew that no women or children lived here. The hallway had cigarette butts on its wooden floor, and newspapers were stacked in piles along the route; the kitchen they passed smelled of stale oil, and its sink was overflowing with dirty dishes; and the living room was ramshackle, crammed with mismatched furniture, stinking of tobacco, with books, magazines, more newspapers, and a desk that contained a computer, brimming ashtrays, laptop, iPad, three cell phones, and a tangled mess of cables. White-ceramic bowls were scattered in various parts of the room, catching droplets of rainwater that were falling from leaks in the ceiling.

Will sat in a chair. "Mr. Lanes—are you well?"

Eddie Lanes removed his sodden jacket, tossed it onto a couch, rubbed his wet hands over his belly, and lit a cigarette. "Are you breaking the ice or hinting I should see a doctor?"

"Breaking the ice."

The journalist asked, "You want a coffee? Maybe something stronger?"

"No, thank you."

"You mind if I fix myself . . . ?"

"Mr. Lanes—this won't take long."

Lanes grabbed his desk chair, swiveled it around, and sat in it. His weight caused the hydraulic seat-height adjuster to sink. "Fucking thing," he muttered as he half stood, adjusted it to the correct height, and sat back down. "What do you want?"

"Information about a man called Viktor Gorsky."

Lanes's eyes narrowed, his hostility replaced by an expression of uncertainty. "Gorsky?"

"The billionaire you were investigating. Why were you investigating him?"

Lanes sucked hard on his cigarette, causing it to burn down to its stub. "Just because you're Thames House doesn't mean I have to talk to you."

"Actually, it does."

"You got proof of who you say you are?"

Will smiled. "Regrettably, if you ring Thames House and ask it to verify the identity of one of its employees, it won't comply." He pointed toward the smeared window, outside of which was the police car. "But by all means telephone that young man's chief constable or the commissioner of the Metropolitan Police. They know I'm here, and they've given me their blessing to speak to you and obtain your cooperation."

Lanes lit another cigarette. "I've not broken any laws."

"To my knowledge, you haven't. And if you had, I wouldn't care. All that matters to me is that police resources are allocated to you to ensure you're kept safe. I know they're not here twenty-four/seven, but it still takes an hour out of their time to drive over here and check you're okay. They could be doing other work. In return for your protection, I would expect you to be cooperative with us."

Lanes tapped his cigarette over the ashtray by his side. "If I tell you what I know, you'll protect my name? That'll be the end of it?"

"I can assure you of the former but not the latter."

"Not the latter?" Lanes frowned.

"Much depends on your level of cooperation."

The journalist placed his hand on top of his computer. "I used to have it all stored in here. But when I got the jitters, I deleted all the files and wiped the hard drive. Everything I know is stored in my head."

Will was silent.

Lanes scratched his stubbly chin, averted Will's gaze for a moment, nodded, and returned his attention to the fake MI5 official. "It started with a bank called Trans Forex."

"I've never heard of it."

"Few have. It was Russian. Very low-profile. Couple of years ago, it went into liquidation. I had a hunch there might be a story in there so started doing some probing. The liquidation records had to be made public, so my starting point was easy. Turns out Trans Forex was bankrolling an offshore company called KapSet and turns out that company is owned by Gorsky. Also turns out Gorsky was a director and shareholder in Trans Forex and is now a director in a very newly established bank called Moscow Vision. Guess what. Moscow Vision is now bankrolling KapSet."

Even though they were several feet apart, Will could smell whiskey on Lanes's breath. He wondered if the smell had come from drinking the night before or this morning. His mind raced as he anticipated seventeen possibilities of where Lanes's information was headed.

Lanes coughed, grabbed a nearby mug, and drank whatever was left inside it. "I spent two years investigating Gorsky after discovering that KapSet was sitting on circa $5 million but seemed not to be trading, aside from occasional payments being made from the balance sheet to companies or persons who for the most part were unnamed. The company's account was always topped back up to 5 million by Moscow Vision, and before that, Trans Forex. I discovered that one of the persons receiving regular, but modest, sums of money was a Bahraini called Arzam Saud."

This was excellent. It was the first possibility Will had not only considered but hoped for. "If KapSet didn't declare the names of the individuals and companies it was paying, how did you ascertain Saud was one of the cash recipients?"

Lanes smiled. "I'm an investigative journalist. I have to be sneaky. Bit like you lot I guess. Saud and Gorsky were coinvestors in some European property deals. The deals were legit as far as I could tell."

"You investigated Saud?"

The journalist nodded. "Young Bahraini man. Inherited money. Thinks a bit too highly of himself as far as I can tell."

"And it occurred to you to check Saud's business records on the long shot that he just might have been one of the guys being paid by KapSet."

"It was a long shot. I had no suspicions. But I thought to

myself, if KapSet ain't telling anyone what it does, what if there are looser tongues among the end users. Saud wasn't as savvy as KapSet. His company and private official returns named KapSet as a payor."

"And you will have asked yourself why Saud needed KapSet money when he was a coinvestor with Gorsky and independently wealthy?"

"Of course. That nagged me. I did some further research. Transpires, the KapSet money were sweeteners to keep Saud in the property deals."

"Sweeteners?"

"Bribes. But there's nothing illegal in that. Leastways, not when you're dealing with Russian and Arab laws that turn a blind eye when money's to be made."

Will didn't articulate what he was thinking. He asked, "How did you get access to KapSet's company records?"

Lanes stubbed out his cigarette, withdrew another, seemed to be contemplating the merits or otherwise of lighting it, said, "Fuck it," to himself and struck a match. After inhaling on the tobacco, he said, "KapSet was registered in the Dubai International Financial Centre. Tax-free zone in the center of Dubai. Officially, DIFC is there to attract banks to set up in the Emirates. Dubai thinks it's going to be the next City of London or Wall Street. It ain't. It's a tart and will drop its panties for anyone. So, it licenses construction companies, oil refineries, consultancies, pretty much anyone who's prepared to pay up for sticking its dick in Dubai. It was easy to find out which DIFC employee was responsible for administering the DIFC legalities of the company's establishment. She was a rather pretty Lebanese woman called Nadia. I made it my business to get to know her."

"Did your employer *The Independent* newspaper know your methods?"

"Methods?"

"You slept with Nadia to get information."

"I didn't say I slept . . ."

"I'm not here to judge, and nor will I breathe a word to the paper that you broke journalistic guidelines. All I'm interested in are facts."

Lanes looked coy. "I brushed myself up. Made myself look better than"—he slapped his chest—"this. Visited a men's grooming salon; put on my best suit; wore a gold watch that was given to me by a politician who wanted to thank me for keeping photos I had of him out of the paper." He patted his gut. "Couldn't do anything about this, though. But that didn't matter. If anything, it helped. In Dubai, if you're fat, you're rich. It's an aphrodisiac."

"So you pretended to be a millionaire. A property developer, I would imagine, because that would give you legitimacy to inquire about KapSet. Perhaps you told Nadia that you were looking to do business with Gorsky's company but wanted KapSet checked out first. You wined and dined her, became intimate with her; she fell for it and wanted to ensure you were doing business with the right people. Giving you that information was harmless, as far as she was concerned. At least, to begin with."

"That about sums it up."

Will was certain he knew the answer to his next question. "And when did the death threats to you start?"

Eddie Lanes glanced at the outside police car, needing reassurance that the cop was still there. "A couple of months after I started probing into KapSet. I can't prove Gorsky was behind it. They were letters sent to my London address. All I was told to do was stop looking into affairs that weren't my business." Lanes looked edgy. "The letters also said that if I ignored their advice, I'd be shot in the head." Water continued to pound the dishes on the floor and other surfaces. "That's everything."

"Not as far as I'm concerned."

The hostility returned to Lanes's face. "I swear that's all I know!"

"I'm sure it is, but there's more to know, and you're going to help me find out what it is."

Lanes looked incredulous. "You can't be serious! You want me to hit the streets again? Put my investigative-reporter hat back on? No way. No *fucking* way!"

Part of Will was conflicted. He could see that Lanes was terrified. But he also thought it was probable that if Lanes stayed here in hiding, he'd drink and smoke himself into an early grave. More importantly, right now, Lanes was Will's only hope of getting closer to Bob Oakland. He could have threatened him again with taking away his safe existence in the Hebrides, but that seemed wholly unfair. Instead, he said, "You can end this. Whether you stay here or return to London, I'm sure you don't want to live the rest of your life looking over your shoulder. I believe I know a way for you to get your life back. But I can't do that for you. Only you can."

"Maybe there'll be no *life* if I go back on the payroll of *The Independent*."

"I'm not asking you to do that." Will stood and handed Lanes a scrap of paper. "That's my cell-phone number. Only you have the number. Call me day or night. I'll pay you very well plus cover your expenses. Tonight, I want you to have a bath and a shave. Take it easy on the booze. Beer or wine is okay, but no hard liquor. And tomorrow, I want you to make yourself look once again like a property tycoon, get on a plane to Dubai, and meet with Nadia."

CHAPTER 12

───────────────────

The Emirates airbus was due to touch down in Dubai in one hour. Inside the business-class section, Eddie Lanes felt resplendent in the peaceful and roomy confines of the cabin. It was, he mused, much like a reading room in a private-members club. People could read, watch, or listen to what they wanted as long as they didn't disturb the person next to them. And there were hostesses on hand to ensure that their passengers' introspective activities were washed down with champagne or other drinks of choice. Lanes could have gotten slowly pickled on the flight. He didn't. He was stone-cold sober. Perhaps it was feeling good and wearing a fine suit that made him decline the offers of booze. The body that normally craved a buzz to get away from reality now felt contented and with purpose. Groves had given him that direction. Lanes didn't buy that Groves was his real name; he also suspected that the man wasn't truthful on any level. That didn't matter. Groves had briefly entered his life, told him what to do, and put him on a plane. It seemed odd it was that simple. A pin bursting a balloon of self-loathing and escapism. Sometime later today, Lanes would have a drink. After all, he wasn't a born-again self-delusional. Vices were locked in him. But he'd have a drink and smile, knowing that he'd worked and deserved a chunk of living and celebrating.

The plane touched down, and shortly after, Lanes was standing outside the Arrivals Section of the airport, thinking that Dubai had mastered fast-track business passenger arrivals but could do nothing to stop the hellish furnace it lived in. He loosened his tie, walked to the taxi rank while pulling his rolling bag, remembered that Emirates Airlines offered a limo service for all of its business-class passengers, thought, fuck it, and grabbed a taxi anyway rather than reenter the airport and wait. Soon, he was getting close to Sheikh Zayed Road, next to which was the Dubai International Financial Centre, its imposing neofascist-design Gate building, and the glitzy high- and low-rises that stretched beyond it for over a mile.

He made a call on his cell.

The woman at the end of the line used foul language that even a hardened journalist like Lanes found shocking.

Twenty minutes later, he was standing on the marble concourse that intersected the Gate's outer walls and the hundreds of offices within them. He blended in. Other businesspeople and DIFC office workers were standing in groups or sitting by water fountains, all of them in suits, most of them having a smoking break. Superficially, the people here and the architecture of the zone were polished examples of how twenty-first-century capitalism should look. But the journalist in Lanes saw through that façade. The vast cluster of buildings seemed to him to be a house of cards; and the predominantly Western men and women loitering in the shade of the Gate's arch carried a nervous air of desperation, as if they'd failed in New York or London, and this place was their last hope to make a pile of easy cash. It was a gold-rush mentality.

He checked his watch—6:00 P.M. He wondered if he was going to be stood up. Then he caught sight of her, walking fast toward him. As ever, she was immaculately dressed and coiffured though the high heels, figure-hugging short skirt, and overly applied makeup were a little too garish for Lanes's tastes. Not that Lanes's tastes counted for anything. Yesterday, he had looked and smelled like a slob. Today, he was just playacting the part of a man who cared about himself.

"Hello, Nadia."

Her face was scowling, her eyes venomous. "You bastard! You've got some nerve turning up here." She continued walking, and Lanes had to skip a few steps to catch up with her and maintain her speed. "I don't want to be seen around here with you."

They walked across a traffic circle, Lanes desperately hoping he didn't break out in a sweat. They were headed toward the twin Emirates Towers, two office high-rises that were as tall as the Empire State Building though more closely resembled the cutting-edge designs found in the new World Trade Center. The walk was only two hundred yards. But in a suit and in summer, the walk could prompt the onset of perspiration that wouldn't desist for an hour. The last time Lanes had been here and had made this walk in the reverse direction, he'd had to visit the Gate's men's room and spend twenty minutes dousing his face with cold water before standing in front of a hand dryer and hoping it would dry his sodden blue shirt.

Heaven only knows how Nadia's thick facial foundation wasn't melting. Perhaps the Lebanese woman was used to the heat.

For Lanes, the feeling accompanied by entering the air-conditioned lobby of the towers was akin to his first sip of liquor after the rare occasions he'd dried out for a month. No, it was better than that. It was bliss. Orgasmic, he decided. Nadia seemed oblivious to the sensation, and kept walking, her expression still angry. Lanes had no idea where she was leading him. That was fine. Nadia had every right to be pissed with him; she was meeting Lanes on her terms.

They reached the glass elevators at the back of the lobby lounge, Nadia pressed number fifty-one on the floor-destination panel, and they entered the elevator. They were alone. As they rose up the tower, catching glimpses of Dubai through the glass windows of the building, Lanes said, "You're looking good."

Nadia replied, "Fuck you."

Neither one uttered another word until they'd reached the top of the building.

They entered Alta Badia Bar, a chic hangout for the wealthy who sip cocktails while sitting on barstools or reclining in sumptuous armchairs while observing the sun go down over Dubai through the building's sloping glass roof cum outer wall. Barely slowing in her stride as she walked past a waiter, she said, "We'll have two Manhattans." She grabbed a chair in the corner of Badia, an area with dim lights and candles on tables, sat, waited for Lanes to sit opposite her, and muttered, "You fucked me, got what you wanted from the DIFC, then vanished."

Lanes put on an expression he hoped looked sheepish and

apologetic. "That's not what happened. Well, the sex bit was true, but I thought you wanted that. Anyway, I didn't vanish. I just had to urgently return to London. I had some business problems to attend to. They've been resolved. I'm back here now, sitting with you."

She picked up a small silver sign on the table showing a picture of a cigarette with a cross over it. She cursed. "Why are you back here?"

"Like I said, to see you."

"Yeah, right."

"It's true, Nadia. I admit, it's not the only reason I'm out of the UK. I've got a huge project under way in Singapore. But I stopped over in Dubai for no other reason than I wanted to say sorry to you."

"Sorry?"

"Yes."

Their drinks arrived, and they sipped their cocktails, a silence between them that was awkward and reflective. When Nadia had finished her drink, she ordered two more and said to Lanes, "After you vanished, I was angry with you. I admitted to the DIFC that I'd shared with you details about Kap-Set's DIFC license and trading activities. I expected them to sack me, but instead they thanked me for my honesty and kept me on."

Lanes had to get Nadia's sympathy. "You were right to do that. But I think after you confessed, someone in DIFC tipped off Viktor Gorsky that I was looking into his affairs." He reached forward and placed his hand on hers.

She recoiled.

"I started getting death threats."

Nadia frowned. "Threats?"

"To my life." He again placed his hand on hers. This time she allowed him to do so. "It wasn't your fault. Out here, it's hard to know whom to trust. But I know I trust you. Nothing that happened was your fault. But it's been a tough few months for me, I have to admit. I was scared. Still am. Jeez, being in Dubai again makes me doubly scared."

"But you still came."

"To say sorry to you."

A trace of a smile emerged on Nadia's face, and the hostility in her eyes receded. "Thank you."

Lanes smiled at her.

After their next drinks were delivered, she asked, "Why would you be threatened? It's not as if anything I told you about KapSet was particularly secret."

Lanes told the truth. "I don't know. I'm missing something."

"Something illegal?"

"Maybe."

Nadia considered this. "I'm authorized to investigate and regulate licensed DIFC companies. If KapSet's withholding something from us, we need to know." She asked, "When do you fly to Singapore?"

"Tomorrow lunchtime."

Nadia looked at the Dubai skyline. Now it was dark, and the flat landscape was filled with a multitude of electric lights. "Would you take me to dinner this evening?"

"I'd love to."

Nadia looked back at Lanes. Her expression was stern. "And what would you like in return?"

Clever Nadia, thought Lanes. "Nothing." It was a lie. But, he couldn't rush things even though time was running out. It wouldn't be until the end of dinner, when he'd plied her with wine, and she'd softened completely, that he'd ask her to supply him with copies of KapSet's DIFC license application and supporting documents.

CHAPTER 13

P atrick was ushered into the Oval Office by an aide who then quickly retreated out of the room. The president was sitting at his desk. In front of him were Donny Tusk and Lieutenant General Jerry Kinnear, the head of the Joint Special Operations Command. Today, Kinnear was in his army uniform, emblazoned with ribbons, and wings, and other special emblems that suggested he'd survived death a thousand times and could kill a man just by looking at him. By contrast, the president and Tusk were in suits, their jackets off and shirtsleeves rolled up.

"Where do I sit?" asked Patrick.

"Wherever you like," replied Tusk.

The CIA officer picked up an office chair and swung it close to Kinnear, causing the general to look at him as if Patrick were being childish. "Might as well sit next to the general, just in case anything bad happens. That way, he can protect me." He smiled at the president. "Good evening, sir."

The president stared at his hand as he repeatedly tapped it against his desk. He looked at Kinnear. "Update."

Kinnear's back was ramrod straight. "We've got drones in the air, satellite surveillance, paramilitary Agency operators on the ground in Iraq and Syria, so they can work their networks of local assets to get information, and I've hunter-killer SF teams ready to move the moment we get hard intel on the CIA officer and translator's location. But so far we've got nothing."

"I see." The president shifted his attention to Patrick and Tusk. "I've not taken the option of moving Saud to Jordan off the table. If I pursue that option, my hope is they hand Saud over to ISIS in exchange for the Jordanian translator and our guy. What do you think, Donny?"

His chief of staff threw his hands up in the air. "Same as you, Mr. President. Even though the Jordanian option is deliberately taking the problem away from us, is it still a compromise to our principle of nonnegotiation with terrorists? I'm losing sleep on that question."

The president looked at Patrick. "And what does the Agency think?"

Patrick considered the question. "The Agency's got thousands of people, none of whom think alike. You won't get a coherent answer from us."

The president nodded. "The issue is not just about principles and tactics. I must also consider *presentation*. And from a *presentational* perspective, there's no doubt that if I hand Saud over to another country, it'll make me look weak and send a clear signal that America will back down to terrorists." He said to himself, "That leaves the hope that General Kinnear's people get lucky, and if not, then we have to let our guy die."

The four men were silent for twenty seconds.

Patrick broke the silence. "I've got a man working the angles outside of Kinnear's frames of reference."

Kinnear looked angry. "Is he any good?"

Patrick smiled while nodding. "With all due respect to you, General, you'd hate him."

Chapter 14

The following morning, it was 8:00 A.M. in Dubai. Lanes was waiting in the Departures Section of Dubai International Airport, frantically checking his watch, while nursing the mother of all alcohol-induced headaches. Even though they'd had a fun evening, now he regretted rolling back into his hotel room at two in the morning. He'd made sure Nadia was dropped off safely at her home before he continued on to the Royal Meridien Hotel, but given that she'd kept pace with his consumption throughout the evening, there was every chance she was still in bed. That wasn't the plan. Last night she promised him that she'd head into DIFC early before meeting him here. She didn't know that he was scheduled to get on a plane to London in an hour rather than waiting here until boarding a lunchtime flight to Singapore. Time was running out.

He sat on one of the rows of metal seats, looking around anxiously. If Nadia didn't turn up, he'd have no choice other than to wait in Dubai for another day. But the MI5 man Groves had told him it was vital he achieved his job and re-

turned today. If Lanes failed to meet that deadline, he wondered if Groves would decide not to pay him. Worse, he
wondered if it would mean Lanes would have no chance of
coming out of hiding without fear that one day a man would
shoot him in the back of the head.

He saw her. Nadia looked exhausted, though, as ever,
she was immaculately dressed. He gave a slight wave as she
looked around at the other end of the concourse. She spotted him, walked quickly to his location, and sat in the empty
seat next to him. She didn't look at Lanes as she said, "I have
it. They're copies, of course, but taken from the originals. It
should be everything you need."

Lanes placed his hand on her arm. "I'm indebted to you."

"Will I see you again?"

Lanes smiled. "I hope so."

She reached into her handbag, withdrew a file, and
handed it to Lanes. "I've got to go before I'm missed at work."
She didn't want people in the airport to think she was with
Lanes, but couldn't stop herself from looking at him one last
time. "I have to deal with businessman all the time as part of
my job. You're not like them. That's why I liked you."

Lanes frowned, and it was on the tip of his tongue to tell
her what he really did for a living. Instead, he squeezed her
arm and said nothing as she got up and left.

When she was out of sight, he opened the file, scan-read
its contents, went to a pay phone and called the number
Groves had given him. It was 4:00 A.M. in London, but
Groves had told Lanes that he could call him day or night.
Groves answered on the third ring. Lanes said, "I'm bringing
them back to the UK. Meet me at the airport. One other

thing: as part of the license application for KapSet to be incorporated into DIFC, Gorsky had to fully declare his background, including any prior military service or criminal convictions. He gave them a photo of his time in the army. It's included in the file."

It had taken Viktor Gorsky and his employees two days to put his mansion and its grounds back to normal after his daughter's wedding. The event had been perfect, and yet, as with all such moments of elation and joy, the aftermath was like a depressing comedown. Doubly so for Gorsky because he had to watch the remnants of the wedding day being slowly dismantled bit by bit until there was nothing left but an old man's home in Tuscany, and the expansive grounds that only he could benefit from.

One of his housemaids jogged through the orchard until she was by his side. "Sir, you have a call. The man says it's urgent."

Gorsky entered one of his home's many living rooms, picked up the handset of the ornate, old-fashioned telephone, and said, "Gorsky."

The caller was a man who worked in the Dubai International Financial Centre. "Our mutual acquaintance has been active again. You were right to keep her employed so that any inquiries into you could be flagged. She's pulled your KapSet files, including the photo of you in the army. I wondered if she'd copied them and given the copies to her English-journalist lover. I've made a few calls to hotels in Dubai. It turns out the journalist was in town, staying at the Royal

Meridien Hotel. But he checked out this morning. The hotel confirmed to me that, right now, he's on a flight to London."

Gorsky ended the call and separately called two other men. One was in the Middle East; the other, Europe. His opening words to both men were identical. "I want you to do something for me. Today."

Nadia said, but he shook his head, 'No, it's the ... The best
people to manage this right now for you are in London.
Elodie...' they had and apparently talked you away
now. Our man in the Middle East, the guy, I mean. He's
going to tell us the exact ... you shouldn't. I want you to see
something for me. I can ...

CHAPTER 15

The plane from Dubai was taxiing toward Heathrow's terminal. During the flight, Eddie Lanes had availed himself of
a few glasses of champagne. With his first sip of champagne
taking place somewhere over Saudi Arabia, Lane had initially
been in a celebratory mood and decided that he would have
one glass for every country he flew over. By the time he'd
reached Eastern Europe, he was buzzing nicely. Then, somewhere over Germany, his mood changed. He'd thought about
Nadia and his manipulation of her to break the rules of her
job. He felt grubby because, though his personal habits at
home were less than desirable and the nature of his job sometimes meant he had to trawl through gutters, Lanes wasn't
by nature a sleaze. In his career, he'd won awards for his in-
sightful and honest scoops; his deceased parents had raised
him to know right from wrong. As his plane had left German
airspace and entered the stratosphere above Belgium, Lanes
decided that he had to meet Nadia again soon and tell her the
truth. The truth, including his real name.

She wasn't attracted to businessmen, didn't want a man's

money, and saw something in Eddie Lanes that she liked. That much was now clear to him. Somehow, in the artificial bubble of Dubai, he'd encountered something real.

But he'd need money to return to see her. By then, Groves would have no use for him and certainly wouldn't be bankrolling his trip. Aside from his temporary role as a spy for MI5, Lanes scraped together a living by selling freelance articles to journals and blogs. Money from them barely covered his monthly Scotch bill. He opened the file Nadia had given him and stared at the photo of a young Viktor Gorsky in the army. This was his paycheck, he decided. He'd give the other documents to Groves and hold on to the photo until such time as he could persuade Groves to pay him extra to hand it over. He replaced the file in his briefcase and shoved the photo in his jacket's inner pocket.

Will Cochrane drove his rental car through the multistory parking lot within the vast complex of Heathrow Airport. Though he was enthused by Lanes's success in obtaining more details about KapSet's registration, he was fully cognizant that the papers the journalist had gotten hold of could be completely irrelevant—Gorsky's association with Saud might have no bearing on the proposed exchange of Bob Oakland for the ISIS terrorist. Patrick was right to be skeptical. Oakland was almost certainly going to be butchered.

But these were the types of risks that Cochrane had taken throughout his career as an intelligence officer. Spies aren't paid to think and act in conventional ways. They have to take a gamble, deal with possibilities, and pursue notions that might appear absurd to many but sometimes produced jaw-dropping success. Trouble is, they can also result in abject failure.

And though his career was deemed remarkable, even by the standards of his superb peers, Will had made mistakes. Some of them had resulted in the deaths of others. He lived with those consequences every day.

He brought the car to a halt in a space, checked his watch, and waited.

Despite being a heaving and sweaty place in the summer, somehow London retains a fresh scent in the air during the warmer months of the year. Perhaps it's due to the frequent westerly breezes that skim across the River Thames, flushing out all things noxious and replacing them with the delicate scent of grass that has been cut in leafy neighboring Oxfordshire. As Eddie Lanes exited passport control and customs, and entered the arrivals section of the airport, he thought he could detect that smell. It should have been impossible to do so. The vast concourse was jammed with people and an assault of pungent odors—chauffeurs holding placards indicating who they were waiting for, their formal attire unconducive to bodies that spent upward of sixteen sweltering hours in the confines of vehicles; passengers physically sick from travel, shuffling toward exits, or bolting to restrooms, their scents identical to those in the latrines of a cruise ship caught in a force-ten hurricane; electric fans in fast-food restaurants, pumping out the aromas of greasy burgers and fries; men and women dashing left and right while hoping their stale smell had been disguised by a few squirts of sample perfumes in the Free shops; and a hundred different nationalities crashing into each other in the confines of one zone, each bringing with them a hint of where they had come from and creating an enticing blend of street smells from Mumbai, New York, Jakarta, Rome, Cairo, Hong Kong, Melbourne, and many other places. Perhaps Lanes's nose was playing tricks on him. It was imagining a smell it wanted. Either way, Lanes was glad to be home.

He was chewing peppermint gum to disguise the champagne fumes though goodness knows why he bothered. It wasn't as if he needed to prove anything to Toby Groves aside from the fact he'd done what the bloody government man had coerced him into doing. Still, Lanes's respect for his self-worth was growing. He didn't want to add the smell of booze to the multitude of other fragrances around him. Until recently, he wouldn't have cared. Now, he told himself he had a woman in his life. This was a turning point. He would chill more about Hamish's sheep, would restore and clean up his home in the Hebrides, would cut out the hard liquor for good, and would invite Nadia to the Isle of Lewis.

He smiled as he followed the signs to the multistory parking lot he'd been instructed to go to. Nadia in Scotland? Would it work? Would she revel in her change of circumstances? Or would she still wear short skirts and totter around while bitching about sheep shit covering her heels? Lanes didn't know because he didn't really know Nadia. But the fantasy of obtaining that knowledge was beguiling and made his blood pump. He felt like a teenage boy, every sense in his body attuned at an optimal level because there was the possibility of happiness that had never before been imagined. Most likely it was all crap. It didn't matter. The notion of the journey did.

It took him a while to find the right level in the parking lot, having gotten confused by Green Zone and Red Zone arrows and different numbers telling him that he was exactly where he should not have been. But when he was on the right level, he moved along the walkway, dodging exhausted travelers pushing carts stacked with cases. Three people were walking in front of him: a sixty-something old Indian woman who was wearing beautiful silks and scarves and was moving at the speed of a snail, no doubt due to exhaustion and the fact her cart must have weighed a ton. Behind her was a Caucasian Englishman similar to her in age, and a younger chauffeur who was carrying the Englishman's baggage. Indian woman and Englishman were not together. The man had expensive clothes, a gold chain visible under his open-neck shirt, gold watch, and good haircut. But all of his finery couldn't disguise the person underneath. Nouveau riche, Lanes decided. Maybe a few million quid under his belt from buying and selling houses. The Indian woman was so dog tired she accidentally veered in front of the man, who seemed hell-bent on getting out of there as fast as possible.

The nouveau riche man shouted, "For fuck's sake!" in a London or Essex accent, and shoved her out of the way with both hands. The Indian woman staggered, tears on her face. "Two fucking months I had to put up with you people in fuckin' Bombay. You can't fucking queue. You can't fucking learn manners," he shouted while walking on with his embarrassed aide. "And my crippled mother walks faster than all of you lot!"

Lanes went to the Indian woman and asked if she was okay. She told him it was her fault. Lanes told her it wasn't; that she'd just encountered the very worst of England. He placed his bag and briefcase on top of her luggage and pushed her cart to the place she wanted to go—a car in the middle of the lot, outside of which her English family members were standing with big welcoming grins on their faces, delighted to see their grandmother from Rajasthan. In the distance, the Englishman was still ranting, his despicable language citing "wogs" and "Pakis" and a whole host of other ignorant labels that sounded completely at home on his hateful lips. What a bastard, thought Lanes.

He then realized that the man was dressed similarly to Lanes. And if he had made his money flipping houses, that brought the oaf into Lanes's pretend line of work. It crystallized in Lanes's mind that this was the last time he ever did anything that wasn't true to his soul.

After retrieving his two bags, in the distance he spotted Groves walking toward him. The oaf who'd abused the Indian lady walked right past Groves while still muttering obscenities. He must have lost his footing because he collapsed to the floor a few yards behind the MI5 man. Funny, though. Groves didn't seem to have noticed, and bizarrely he seemed oblivious to the oaf's chauffeur shouting that he needed help because his employer might be having a heart attack. Instead, Groves kept his eyes on Lanes and continued walking, a smile on his face.

Of course. Groves had seen what the oaf had done to the Indian woman. With a lightning-fast, powerful sleight of hand, he'd delivered justice.

The act made Lanes view Groves in a wholly different light.

The man he'd assaulted slowly and painfully got to his feet. Now, he was mute. He limped onward with his chauffeur.

The MI5 man was eighty yards away, his face and most of his body was partially obscured by stationary vehicles. He must have driven here, Lanes guessed; most likely in some nondescript car that drew little or no attention. Lanes wouldn't be using the car because after this was done he'd return into the airport and take a domestic flight to Glasgow. There, he'd stay in a hotel for the night before making the journey back to his home on the islands.

He saw Groves more clearly now though his face was still obscured. He wondered how much cash the MI5 officer would pay for the photo. At least a couple of grand, he decided. He yanked his suitcase over the lip of a sidewalk and, as he did so, he felt excruciating pain in his lower back. At first, he thought he might have torn a muscle. But in the space of one second, the pain increased to a level where he thought he might black out. Someone behind him grabbed his briefcase. But Lanes still held on to it, and was spun around by whoever was pulling on his bag. A man was before him, wearing shades and a sweater with its hood covering most of his head. A mugger? Something flashed by the man's free hand. A knife. It went straight into Lanes gut.

The man prized the briefcase away from Lanes, turned, and ran, dodging between cars until he was out of sight. Lanes twisted around, released his bag, clutched the wound in his stomach, and staggered toward the place he'd last seen

Groves. Blood covered his fingers, and more of it was dribbling out of his mouth. His eyes were screwed up, his body shaking, and a piercing ringing was in his ears; and the pain, my goodness, the pain. Groves came into view, his expression immediately turning to shock when he saw the journalist.

The MI5 officer sprinted toward him. "What happened?!" He cradled Lanes as the journalist fell backward.

Lanes couldn't speak. He just stayed on his back, Groves's arms underneath him, the officer looking in quick succession at his stomach wound and face. It took all of Lanes's willpower to do it, but he managed to move his arm and pull the photo of Gorsky out of his jacket. Still clutching the photo, his hand dropped to his chest.

"Stay with me. I'll get you help!" said Groves while desperately looking around.

When he glanced back at Lanes, the journalist was dead.

CHAPTER 16

Nadia entered her apartment on level ten of Amwaj 3, a thirty-three-story apartment block in Dubai's Jumeirah Beach Residence complex. She was conflicted as to whether to fix herself a coffee to try to wake herself up after her awfully long day at work, a shift that had seemed like a week because her hangover had gotten progressively worse. She decided caffeine wouldn't help her one bit and opted to make a multivitamin drink. She dropped her bag onto the small breakfast table where she always dined alone and went into her kitchen. Normally, this was a room where she enjoyed making Lebanese food while sipping a glass of wine. Now, the prospect of cooking and alcohol made her feel nauseous. If she was still awake, in an hour she'd order a pizza and ice-cold Coke.

Drink in hand, she walked across her tastefully decorated yet minimalist living room, pulled open the sliding windows, and stepped onto her balcony. Sitting by her wrought-iron garden table, she sipped her drink and watched people strolling on the beach below, some of them moving ankle deep along the sea's edge while enjoying the calming influence that dusk seemed to bring to the less hectic outskirts of the city. Maybe later, she'd go down there with the hope that a stroll would make her feel human again. Perhaps not. Her best option was to go to bed and just get this day over with.

Had yesterday been worth the pain of today? She thought so. Though she'd initially wanted to strangle him, it had been nice to see Edward Panes. He'd been charming over dinner, kept reiterating that he was seeing her to say sorry and that she should rest assured that the very last thing on his mind was to try to get her into his bed. As the evening had progressed, the more she thought she liked him. Probably that was the influence of the alcohol. Or loneliness. For all of its parties, and clubs, and activities, and tax-free lifestyles, Dubai was one of the loneliest places on the planet if you were an individual who had depth of character. By contrast, *the shallows*, as she called them, just loved it here—partying, making hordes of friends just like them, getting rich, spending it all, the husbands thinking they'd become Rockefeller, their wives carving up their days with coffee mornings, tennis matches, sex with their tennis instructors, and all the time treating their impoverished servants like slaves. People like Nadia spent every day in Dubai wishing she was somewhere where grass grew naturally and one could dip one's feet in water that wasn't as hot as a bath. The shallows, on the other hand, embraced their new lifestyle, right up to the moment the party would inevitably come to a crashing halt. Marriages would turn sour, jobs got lost, money would run out, and the shallows would inevitably return to their tiny homes in England or wherever and realize that they were no longer lords and ladies of the manor. In fact, they were once again who they always had been. Trash.

Nobody stayed here long term. The question was whether you left on your terms or Dubai's terms. If she stayed, Nadia knew her life would either become more introverted, or she'd have no choice than to join the ranks of shallow, good-time idiots. Either would be hell. But she had no home in Lebanon anymore. Her parents were dead, and her siblings were grown-up and had families of their own. Like many Lebanese do, all of them had left their home country.

By now, she guessed that Edward was close to landing in Singapore, if that's really where he was headed. And was Edward Panes his real name? After she'd first met him, and he'd had sex with her and subsequently disappeared, she'd Googled his name to find out more about him. There were lots of people with that name listed on the Internet. Some of the links showed photos and vocations. None of them matched the man she'd slept with. Thing was, though, there were so many false people in the Emirates. Edward was just yet another. It had become almost de rigueur for people in Dubai to exchange made-up names and lie about their vocations. But what got her about Edward was that she thought he didn't want to be like that. Over dinner, he'd spoken with intricate precision and insight about the machinations of British politics and its marriage of convenience to the UK's media. And he'd asked her many questions about her life and aspirations. In her experience, male businessmen in Dubai would almost always take up the lion's share of dinner with a lady by talking about themselves and how much money they were making.

She supposed she'd never hear from him again. He was

out of here. That was all that mattered to him. Lucky man, to be out of here. Still, the foolish and impetuous side of her wished she'd gotten on a plane with him. Maybe when they landed in Singapore, they'd have parted company. Who knows? It would have been worth it to find out.

She gulped the rest of her vitamin drink and headed into her bedroom, adjacent to which was an en suite bathroom. After turning on the shower, she closed the bedroom curtains so she couldn't be observed by occupants of the other towers in the neighborhood and to shut out Dubai. Right now, she wanted to be alone, to wash, to sleep, and maybe in doing so start making plans about her future. Nobody else was going to make those plans for her. Perhaps she'd move to London. That's where Edward said he lived. Another foolish dream.

She sighed, opened her wardrobe, and screamed.

A man was inside.

Tall.

Caucasian.

Staring straight at her.

He punched her in the face with sufficient force to throw her body onto the bed. She held her hands to her bloody nose while kicking wildly through the air with her feet. She was about to cry for help, but the man wrenched her arms away from her face, thrust her bed's pillow on her mouth, and put his full body weight behind his hand. She lashed, punched, and scratched at the man's arms and body, but he held her firm, pressing even harder as he squeezed the life out of her.

No air in her lungs, which were now convulsing in agony.

Her mind was exploding.

Eyes and throat, too.

It felt like an hour, but in one minute her body gave one final convulsion, her back arched, and Nadia was dead.

Signor Gorsky was tasting a glass of Argiano Solengo while listening to Igor Stravinsky's *The Rite of Spring* on his living room's CD player. The red wine was an extremely good vintage and had been difficult to obtain. He was pleased that for the most part it met his exacting standards though the taste was not quite right on the receptor cells in the center of his tongue. His telephone rang. He left it unanswered as he never picked up a phone unless he knew exactly who was calling. Before she'd left home to pursue married life, many times his daughter had purchased cell phones for him and showed him how to add contacts so that their names appeared on the screen when they rang. All of the phones were in a drawer, unused.

His housekeeper walked quickly into the room, answered the phone, nodded, and held it toward her boss. "It's okay, sir. One of your associates."

The old Russian got to his feet and walked to the phone. "Yes?"

"It's done. Both business transactions have been successfully executed."

"Excellent."

"But there's a problem. The photograph of old business was not among the paperwork. Maybe it's been given to someone who shouldn't have it."

Gorsky asked, "You're sure?"

"I checked the case many times. It was possible the photo was on his person, but I didn't have time to search him. The location was too public. Plus, there was a tall man walking toward the place where it was done. I'd earlier spotted him waiting nearby. There was something about him I didn't like. It was too risky to hang around."

Gorsky was silent for five seconds. "We must assume the photo was handed to that person or someone like him. You're of no use to me now in London. I want you to go to Moscow and keep an eye on the last of them. You know who I'm referring to?"

"Yes. That loose end should have been permanently tied up long ago."

"Ah, but I am a sentimental when it comes to old memories. But my sentimentality has its limits. Call me again if anything happens. I'll issue you fresh instructions."

Gorsky replaced the handset in its cradle, walked back to the sumptuous arrangement of armchairs, rugs, and sofas, and sat down. Stravinsky's music filled the vast room. He tasted his wine again. It was now perfect. He decided that was because it had been allowed to breathe.

CHAPTER 17

Just one mouthful of the gruel made Ramzi spit it out, and exclaim, "What is that?"

The jihadist who was crouching before him and attempting to feed the insipid white food to his prisoner was the short yet broad-shouldered deputy of the six-man Chechen unit. He smashed the bowl into Ramzi's face, covering it with globules.

In the far corner of the room, Bob Oakland thrashed against his bonds and chain. "Please don't! He didn't mean it! Please, I beg you!"

The jihadist was silent as he unclipped the translator's neck chain from its lock on the wall, and dragged Ramzi to his feet. The Jordanian was shaking his head furiously, trying to get the soup out of his eyes and mouth. "I'm sorry! So sorry. I didn't mean . . ."

The Chechen yanked the chain, forcing Ramzi's bound ankles to move his feet in an inch-by-inch shuffle across the dead room. Ramzi was crying, moaning in despair, and kept looking at Bob. "Mr. Oakland. Say something clever. Make them stop. I beg you."

But Bob had no clever words, only ones that instead would have made him sound like a groveling beggar, his pleas being trampled on by men who viewed him as pathetic for stooping so low. "Be strong, Ramzi," was all he could think to say though he meant every word.

When the guard and prisoner were out of the room, and the door was slammed shut, Oakland lowered his head and prayed to God, asking him to be merciful and put a bullet in Ramzi's brain. He'd never prayed before. But this was important; he thought God might listen even though Bob had been rude enough not to reach out to him before. He looked at the ropes that were lashed around his ankles. They'd cut into his skin so regularly that he was sure his legs would carry permanent reminders of his bonds. If he survived his ordeal of imprisonment, he'd have another story to tell, he thought. Did I tell you how I got all these scars? Yes, Grandpa, a thousand times. Wanna hear it again? Yes please!

Ramzi's screams and shouts were unmistakable from the room next door. There was banging, most likely from his head being smashed against the wall. It had happened so many times to both prisoners. But there were also knives, other instruments, and a bucket in that room. So far they'd not been used. But so far Ramzi and Bob had done everything the guards had told them to do.

A fly landed on the rope wounds on his legs. He tried to shake the fly off, but it kept landing back on his flesh. "Don't lay eggs," said Bob to the fly. "*Please*. Don't lay eggs in there."

CHAPTER 18

The detective in Heathrow Airport's police station stopped writing and looked at Will Cochrane across the desk in the bare interview room. "Mr. Groves—you've nothing else to add?"

Will shrugged. "Like what?"

The detective reread the statement he'd taken from the sole human witness to Eddie Lanes's murder. "You didn't know the victim?"

"Correct."

"You were in Heathrow to meet an American colleague?"

"Yes. Like I said, it was only when I arrived that I got his message that he'd missed his flight."

"And you never saw the killer?"

"I didn't. Will the CCTV video you have of the murder be sufficient to identify him?"

"Not likely. But DNA's a miracle cure for crime these days."

Will suspected they'd never catch the killer that way.

"We're going to need to take your DNA as well. You held

Lanes. We got that on camera as well. You okay with our taking samples from you?"

"No problem."

The detective slid the handwritten statement and a pen across the desk. "Okay. Just initial each page and sign and date at the end. If we need you again, we'll get in touch. You may need to appear in court as a witness if it gets to trial. Possibly not, though. You didn't actually see the murder."

"Happy to oblige." Will signed the document while looking at the detective and making rapid assessments about the man. Thirty-five; made detective recently; divorced; remarried; regretted doing so; was once a smoker but quit at least four months ago; is on a diet that requires him to fast twice a week; and supports Arsenal soccer club. "I don't suppose you know the score from today's match?"

The detective frowned. "Which match?"

"Arsenal v Everton. I'm a Gunners supporter. Would hate to see Everton even get a draw with my team."

The detective grinned while withdrawing a soccer ticket that was previously partially exposed in his jacket pocket. "I support Arsenal, too." His smile vanished as he flicked the ticket. "Sorry to say we lost out. The Toffees kicked our asses. Three nil."

"Shit."

"My sentiments exactly."

Will shook his head. "When I got job promotion twelve months ago, I was given a VIP pass to Arsenal games. I thought I was given a pass to Heaven. Seems I was wrong."

"What do you do for a living?"

Will replied, "I'm an academic. I'm not a medically trained

oncologist, but I specialize in the study of cancer. Am I allowed to smoke in here?"

"No. We used to allow it but not anymore."

Will pretended to look frustrated. "Just as well I quit. My wife busted my balls about it. Said I couldn't study cancer and smoke at the same time. It made sense, and I listened to her. It was the only thing she said that felt right. Everything else was nuts. Still, I kept going back to her for some reason. I wish I wasn't that weak."

The detective was silent, trying to hide signs that he knew exactly how Will felt.

Will breathed in deeply and adopted an expression that suggested he was back in the here and now and transcending personal reflection. "You're ambitious?"

"Yeah. Well, I tell myself I am." The detective looked pissed off. "Heathrow wasn't my choice. All I get here is guys and gals who've smuggled in an extra carton of fags, and drug mules whose jaundice makes them stand out a mile when they stagger through the Nothing To Declare customs aisle. It's when the condoms in their asses rupture and release the drugs into their systems that they turn that color. There's no challenge in spotting them."

"But now you have a murder to investigate."

The detective's eyes glistened. "Yes."

"Can I see the CCTV footage again?"

"Sure." The detective tapped on his laptop keyboard, swiveled the computer so that its screen could viewed by both men, and pressed Play. There was Eddie Lanes in the parking lot, pulling his bag over the lip of a sidewalk. Will wasn't in view. A tall man appeared on the left of the screen, wearing jeans, boots, sunglasses, and a grey sweater with its hood up. He plunged his knife into Lanes's back, grabbed his briefcase, spun him around, stuck his knife into his gut, prized the case off the journalist, and ran. Moments later, Will was on the scene.

Will said, "Go back to the bit where the man first appears."

The detective rewound the footage and pressed Play again. "Stop."

The detective did as he was told, pausing the video on the moment the killer was about to make his first strike.

"Do you notice anything about the way the killer approaches Lanes?"

The police officer frowned. "Nothing odd."

"He doesn't run at him; nor does he use stealth. It's more like a cocky saunter."

"He's done this before?"

Will completely agreed though he didn't answer because he didn't want the detective to know that he was doing anything other than playing at amateur detective. Nor did he want the man to know that Will was helping him crack his first murder case. "He approaches Lanes like a strutting cockerel that's approaching its opponent in a cockfight. His walk is muscular, but there's also self-assured rhythm in his footing, a rhythm that's necessary to ensure his upper body is perfectly poised to make its attack. Where've you seen movement like that before?"

The detective's eyes narrowed. "Maybe a boxing ring."

"Excellent."

"After the first bell to round one rings, he's circling his opponent, almost floating, ready to spring."

"You're making a fine detective. Now, press Play again, then stop it after he prizes the case off Lanes. Watch what happens."

When the detective stopped the video, he said, "I don't see anything."

"The killer might be a boxer. But when he spins Lanes around, the killer swings his arms to create momentum that wholly off balances Lanes. The killer steps in close, shifts his hips, and twists Lanes's arm upward, putting it in an agonizing lock. That in itself would have been sufficient for the assailant to successfully force Lanes to drop his case." Will nodded at the screen. "When I was younger, I did some mixed-martial-arts training. One of my kick-smoking-and-get-fit phases of life. These moves remind me of someone who's had the same training."

The detective leaned in close to the screen. "You're right. A mixed martial artist. Probably he does it to keep him in top form for his day job, which is . . ." He hesitated.

"I'm not thinking mugger. Even the dumbest of robbers would know there are infinitely better places to randomly rob someone and get away with it. This man wanted Lanes's case—*only* Lanes's case."

"And even though he got the case, he killed Lanes anyway, so the victim couldn't identify him."

"Or he was paid by someone to execute Lanes. If I were you, I'd look at the membership of mixed-martial-arts clubs. Start in London. Check whether any members have convictions, but also look for military combat history."

"Why military?"

Will shrugged, careful not to appear too convincing in

what he was saying. "Just a guess. I haven't a clue about these things. But I'm thinking this through logically, much in the same way that I approach my work when I look at cancerous cells. What if this guy's a contract killer? Maybe his employer doesn't want to use someone who's spent time in prison for serious assault or murder because that type of person's profile might lead police to the employer. But the same employer might decide that an ex-military guy for hire might prove just as useful, maybe more so. Just a thought."

The detective grinned. "Mr. Groves, you're in the wrong job." He stood and shook Will's hand. "You've been really helpful. We won't bother you again unless we have to."

"I'll send you some tickets to watch *The Gunners* if you catch the guy."

The detective's eyes lit up. It had been unprecedented for him to interview a witness to a crime who had so much in common with him. And Groves's observations had given the detective a major starting point in the murder case. It had been a pleasure to encounter such a cooperative member of the public. As a result, he'd ensure that the police didn't bother Groves again unless absolutely necessary.

Not that the police would be able to contact Groves again. He didn't exist. And Will's DNA samples would be of no use. There wasn't a DNA base in the world that had records of a sample belonging to a man called Will Cochrane.

O ne hour later, Will called from a pay phone in Heathrow's Terminal 5. "Lanes is dead. Someone knifed him and stole the papers he was bringing me from Dubai. But not everything's lost." He told him about the photo that Lanes had managed to withdraw from his jacket, so Will could take it. Given he was on the brink of death, it had been an extremely brave thing that Lanes had done.

The photo was of Gorsky serving as a lieutenant in the 9th Company, 345th Independent Guards Airborne Regiment, during the Soviet-Afghan war. It was an official Soviet photo, had Gorsky's name under his image, and Cyrillic handwriting in the corner saying, *Me, two days before shrapnel put me on my ass and into civilian life—V. Gorsky.*

Will said, "I need you to do something for me fast. You might need to liaise with your DIA," the United States Defense Intelligence Agency, "or maybe the information I need is in your databases. Either way, I'll call you back in one hour."

When Will called Patrick back in that time frame, he listened to the CIA officer say, "Got it. Name and address."

Will committed the details to memory.

"What are you going to do next?"

Will glanced at the nearby flight departures board. He was in Terminal 5 for a reason. It was the terminal used for departures to Russia. Patrick's information had confirmed Will was right to put himself here. "I'm getting on a flight to Moscow."

CHAPTER 19

During his journey to Moscow, Will had eschewed offers of food and drink, had not touched the inflight entertainment, and instead had sat motionless, thinking about Eddie Lanes's death. So often in his line of work, the imperative to rescue one individual resulted in the demise of another. Each time, he told himself that he had no way of predicting his assets' downfalls; and yet he also knew full well that if he hadn't entered their lives, there was every possibility they would still be alive. Will Cochrane sent people to their deaths, he frequently concluded. He was like a judge of old, who would place a black cloth cap on his head before pronouncing to a petrified prisoner in the docks that he would be hanged until dead.

He couldn't know for sure that someone in DIFC would realize that Nadia had copied the KapSet registration files and report that to Viktor Gorsky. As a result, it was impossible for him to predict with certainty that a killer would be unleashed to murder Lanes. But Will Cochrane knew all the possible outcomes of his work before he made his first move on his figurative chessboard. What had happened in Dubai and London was one possible sequence of events that could follow his entry into Lanes's house in the Hebrides. It made him feel shitty and angry with himself.

If he'd just been a few yards closer to Lanes in the parking lot, things could have been different. Or not. The man who attacked Lanes knew exactly what he was doing. Will had been telling the truth when he told the Heathrow detective to look for an unarmed-combat expert who was ex-military. If Will was a gambling man, he'd have bet the Lanes's murderer was ex–Special Forces.

He took a taxi from the airport and stared out the window. He'd been to Moscow many times and knew it as well as he knew London. It was a city where he'd suffered pain and joy, had made the very best of friends and worst of enemies, shot and kidnapped high-value targets, rescued men and women, and seen some of his brave colleagues being beaten to the ground by rifle butts and dragged off in an army vehicle to be tortured. None of it had happened during the height of the Cold War. It had all taken place when Russia was momentarily best pals with the West. That veneer of bullshit had subsequently slipped. It made Moscow an even more dangerous place for a man like Will Cochrane to be.

The taxi turned into Ul. Marshala Poluboyarova, in the residential and commercial suburbs of the city's southeastern outskirts. After paying the driver and waiting until the taxi had disappeared, Will walked a hundred yards and stopped. On the other side of the street were apartment blocks and residential houses. He stood on the sidewalk as a fine rain began to descend, cars on the street driving slowly, some of them with their headlights on even though it was late morning. There were people on the streets though not many. Most of them were solitary, moving quickly with their hands in their pockets and hoods and collars pulled up to shield them from the weather. A break in the clouds introduced a scythe of sunlight illuminating the fine drizzle of rain droplets, its long blade touching the earth and moving with the shift in clouds. As the clouds became still, the scythe was motionless, pointing at Will and the house he was observing.

He waited for a gap in the traffic, so he could cross the street and knock on the door. He looked left and right along the route and glanced back at the house. An old man emerged from the property. He was wearing a thick overcoat even though the temperature wasn't cold, a wide-brimmed hat, and carried a cane to compensate for his limp. Will subtly looked at his surroundings, walked across the road, and followed the man.

They walked for several hundred yards along the side of the road, the old man moving slowly, Will matching his pace from fifty yards behind. All the time, Will examined the handful of people they passed—a construction worker with arthritis, a housewife who was heading to shops, an off-duty cop who was in trouble at work, and a junior civil servant who could no longer bear the mundanity of his work. Though he'd never seen them before, Will knew that's who they were.

On the other side of the street, behind Will's field of vision, was another man whom Will had previously seen, albeit on CCTV footage in London. He was tall, had a powerful athletic frame, and was wearing sunglasses and a grey sweater with its hood pulled up. He was watching the old man and the person following him, certain that neither of them was aware of his presence.

The old man entered Kuzminsky Park; previously a nine-hundred-acre nineteenth-century estate owned by Prince Golitsyn, now it was a peaceful expanse of grass and trees within which were the ruins of a palace, bathhouse, other neoclassical buildings, gates, iron fences and lions, pavilions, and a stable yard with sculptures of horses. Will had been here before to conduct a brush contact with an SVR agent. That was a long time ago. Now, he couldn't yet decide if the old man was walking through the park to reach another destination or whether he was here to get some exercise and soak up the peaceful ambience.

It was the latter, Will decided, when he saw the old man stop, pull out some bread from his coat pockets, and toss chunks of it into the adjacent pond, where ducks paddled and squawked in a sound that resembled hysterical human laughter. The Russian sat on a metal bench, both hands clasped over the top of his cane, staring at the waterway. Will glanced around, walked quickly toward him, and sat next to the man.

"Good morning, sir," said Will in Russian.

The man lifted the rim of his hat and looked at Will. "Good morning." His thin face was clean-shaven, and a scar was on his chin.

"The day would be better without the rain, I think."

"I *know* it would be better." The old man made ready to leave.

"Mr. Mikhaylov—please stay for a moment."

The Russian was visibly suspicious. "How do you know my name? Who are you?"

Will had thought about who he wanted to be when meeting the old man. There were manifold false identities he could have used, but only one brought with it justice and closure. "My name is Eddie Lanes. I'm a journalist with the British newspaper *The Independent* though I'm here in a freelance capacity."

"Journalist?" Mikhaylov's evident suspicion remained. "Your Russian is perfect."

"I was based with our Moscow bureau for a number of years."

The man huffed and jabbed his cane on the paved sidewalk. "You could be Russian secret police, trying to trick me."

"I'm not. But if I ask you anything that makes me sound like a liar, walk away. I won't bother you again."

"What do you want?"

"Just information. *Old* information." Will's eyes imperceptibly took in details about the man—his coat was frayed at the cuffs; a tear in its sleeve had been stitched and restitched many times; there were spots of blood on the collar that its owner had attempted to remove, first with cold water, then with cheap vodka; the spots were recent, and ranged in age from weeks ago to a day old; his mottled facial skin betrayed a penchant for vodka though of late he'd stopped drinking altogether, maybe through conviction, more likely due to fear about his ill health; shoes that were once pristine were now ragged, yet still highly polished, and had been resoled at least six times; his suit smelled of mothballs, and had only recently been taken out of its wardrobe after decades of no use.

There were eighteen other indicators that told Will that Mikhaylov was a poor man who couldn't afford medical care and was determined to see out his end with dignity. "I have an expenses budget for my story. If you can help me, I'll pay you $5,000."

The suspicion evaporated from the Russian's face. "That's a lot of money."

"I'm hoping to sell the report to the *New York Times* or one of the British tabloids. They pay well."

Mikhaylov rubbed his scar. "I can't say I don't need the money. But I'm not sure I'll be of any use to you. I don't think I've got anything interesting to say. My life's been fairly unremarkable."

"Maybe once that wasn't true." Will glanced around. They were alone. "I'm doing an investigative feature on a man called Arzam Saud."

"The prisoner in the news? The one the terrorists want released?"

"That's him. It's topical news right now." Will shrugged, hoping he looked unthreatening and nonchalant. "I'm looking into Saud, trying to do a human-angle story on him. Who is he? What makes him tick? What turned the young man toward terrorism? That kind of stuff."

Mikhaylov smiled. "Just write one line—*Arzam Saud turned crazy.* That should sum it all up."

"I'm hoping there's a bit more flesh on the bone than that." Will also smiled. "Though you might have nailed the truth. They're all crazy."

"Maybe, but I don't know Saud or anyone like him."

"I didn't expect you to." Will checked again to ensure they weren't being watched or overheard. "What interests me is his business association with Viktor Gorsky."

"Gorsky?"

"He's a very private man. I'm having a devil of a job finding out about Gorsky's background. I'm hoping that's where you can help." He withdrew the photo that Lanes had given him. It was smeared with the journalist's dried blood. "This was Gorsky when he was in the Soviet Army. Looks to me like the shot was taken in a combat zone or lookout fortification. Gorsky was in an airborne unit. Maybe he was working in a four- or eight-man team. Judging by what he wrote at the bottom of the photo, he was invalided out of the zone two days later because of an injury from an artillery or mortar strike." He handed Mikhaylov the photo.

The old man stared at the image, his frail hand shaking and his eyes watering, as he said, "My goodness, that was a long time ago. Why is there blood on the photo?"

"I had a nosebleed while studying the image. You were Gorsky's captain, yes?"

"Yes."

"And I suspect this was taken when the Soviet Army was advancing or retreating in the Afghan mountains during the war there in the 1980s."

"Correct." Mikhaylov ran a finger across the image. "In fact, there were six of us there. It *was* an advance lookout post, high up in the mountains. Our job was to spot Afghan troop movements and relay those movements to command. Sometimes we were ordered to engage any Afghan advances if our troops couldn't get there in time. We had a name for that tactic—*Suicide*. This photo was taken two days before our last suicide engagement in the region. It went badly wrong. We thought we were hitting a small skirmishing party. Then

Afghan armor appeared. They hit our position with everything they had. Were it not for our bunkers and Soviet reinforcements arriving later, we'd have been obliterated. Still, Gorsky got severely clipped." His finger rested on the official Soviet photo of a man in combat uniform; underneath his image was his name in type. "I can confirm that the man you see in the photos is Viktor Gorsky."

"What happened after the assault?"

Mikhaylov's voice trembled as his memory took him back to Afghanistan. "We were exhausted, our minds weren't working, nobody could hear because of the bombardment. We'd managed to hold off the Afghan advance for two hours until we were relieved by hundreds of our men, who were supported by airstrikes. Most of the Afghans were killed, the others retreated. When it calmed down, four KGB officers came to our position and asked us if any of us had died in the battle. I told them, no, but that one of us was on the brink of death unless he received urgent medical treatment. I pointed at Gorsky."

Will handed Mikhaylov a brown envelope containing cash that had been meant for Lanes by way of payment for what he'd done in Dubai. "Do me a favor: Take a different route home, and if anyone asks, you never came to the park today."

"Why?"

Will didn't answer. "What happened to Gorsky?"

The old man stuffed the envelope inside his jacket. "The KGB took him away, and I've never seen him since."

Will frowned. "You must have seen Gorsky on television or in the papers. He's now a powerful businessman."

"You mean the billionaire Gorsky? The property developer?"

"The recluse who's done business with Arzam Saud."

The old man shrugged. "He may share the same name, but that's not the Viktor Gorsky I knew. My eyesight is not what it was. But as far as I'm concerned, the businessman you reference looks more like the highest-ranking KGB officer who came to the mountains after our battle than the man who I served alongside."

The killer who'd followed Mikhaylov and Will could easily see the two men from his hidden position on the other side of the pond. Holding his binoculars in one hand, he used the other to call Gorsky. He told his boss what he could see. "The tall man with Mikhaylov is one hundred percent the same man I saw walking toward Lanes, before I killed him. I'm in no doubt that he's a special operative. Probably British or American."

Viktor Gorsky's response to the former Russian Spetsnaz commando was immediate. "Kill the operative. Then go to the old man's house and put him out of his misery."

Will watched Mikhaylov hobble away. The retired army officer had done what Will had asked him to do, taking a different route out of the park. It was a perfunctory precaution. Anyone who wanted him dead could easily get to the old man at his home or elsewhere. Once again, Will felt he'd entered someone's life and ruined it. This cycle had to end. His mind raced because of Mikhaylov's certainty that the man in the photo was not the man who'd submitted the photo alongside KapSet's other DIFC registration documentation. The truth was that Viktor Gorsky was a former senior KGB officer who'd assumed the identity of a soldier called Gorsky. He'd wanted a dead casualty after the Afghan assault. When none was forthcoming, he'd taken the next best thing—an injured soldier. No doubt he'd taken the wounded paratrooper to a remote mountain gully in Afghanistan and shot him in the back of the head.

Will checked his watch. He had to get out of Russia. He started walking back along the route he'd taken in the park and used his cell phone to call Patrick. "Tell the president that he must not make any decisions about Saud. Not without me present."

Patrick tried to object.

But Will interrupted him. "Just do it. I'm on the next available flight to D.C."

The former Russian Special Forces operative shoved his binoculars into his jacket and sprinted between trees and alongside dense foliage. His target—the operative who'd just met with Mikhaylov—couldn't see him. He withdrew a knife similar to the one he'd used to end Eddie Lanes's life. Its blade was sturdy and razor-sharp. In the hands of a child, it could easily kill an adult as powerfully built as the man he was going to murder. In the Russian's hand, the blade could make a man unrecognizable as a human being.

Even with no weapons, the Russian's combat expertise

was such that time and time again he'd been able to use his hands, feet, knees, and other body parts to make men and women's bones break, their hearts stop, and their brains shut down forever.

He stopped close to a clearing at the easterly end of the pond. Crouching to one side of a bush, he saw the operative talking on his cell phone as he walked along the park's footpath. The man was oblivious to the nearby predator. That was a bonus though the Russian would have been equally comfortable meeting him head-on. That would happen two hundred yards ahead of the man. There was a cluster of trees that obscured the path within them. A perfect place to dispatch the operative. He moved fast along the tree line, needing to get ahead of his prey and close to the kill zone. The next time he'd see him, the killer would be looking into his eyes while twisting the blade of his knife in his gut.

Everything now made sense to Will. When Patrick had sat next to him in London's Royal Albert Hall and told him about Saud, Will had responded that he had to construct a starting point to the mission that was outside of conventional thinking. Patrick had countered with skepticism, saying Will's position was fine so long as he had an idea where such an unconventional approach might lead. Will remembered what he had told Patrick.

I've several hypotheses as to where it could lead, and one in particular fascinates me.

It had fascinated him. And now he was convinced it was the truth.

He kept on walking, deciding that he'd head to Kuzminka Metro Station and take the train back to the airport.

The Russian breathed deeply and silently as he reached his kill zone. He'd sprinted to get there, moving over rough land, hiding within the cover of trees and bushes. The target would arrive in seconds. Soon, he'd have sight of him again. He wondered how hard the man would resist his inevitable death. Probably, he'd react like a wounded lion. Desperate. Savage. Undisciplined. Like the big-game animals of bygone days who'd been lured to a tethered goat, only to be caught unawares by a hunter with a rifle. He smiled, gripping his knife.

The knee that punched into the base of his spine knocked him forward, but the hand that then gripped his throat made his upper body stay still while the momentum of his legs carried onward. His target was over him, squeezing his gullet and pushing him to the ground. The Russian kicked his side, wrapped his other leg around his neck, ready to move his leg sideways and flip the target away, and plunged his knife at the man's belly.

But the man dodged the blade, grabbed the Russian's knife-wielding hand with his thumb on the upper side and fingers underneath, and twisted his hand while looking into his eyes and calmly saying, "No."

The word and accent were English.

An Englishman.

The Russian hated Englishmen.

They were so effete.

The Russian kept pushing his leg against the man's neck. It was a move that put anyone away in the judo component of his beloved mixed martial arts. But the man on top of him remained stock-still. Immobile.

The Englishman broke the Russian's wrist with a rapid snap, dropped quickly, and wrapped one arm around the Russian's neck, the other was outstretched, blocking the killer's free arm. He tightened his bicep around the Russian's throat, squeezing as slowly and assuredly as a boa constrictor, one leg cocked at a forty-five-degree angle flush against the heathland underneath, the other ramrod straight and pointing away from the men. The legs were counterbalances and grips, adding to the impossibility of escape.

But the Russian struggled anyway.

His target held him in his viselike grip. In a soothing voice, he whispered, "Don't struggle. You know it delays matters."

The Russian slapped his hand repeatedly on the ground. It was instinctual, like his opponents had done many times on the dojo mat of his MMA class in his club in south London. It meant, *Release me, I give up.*

Will Cochrane didn't give up. Not until the Russian went limp and was dead.

CHAPTER 20

When the six jihadists entered the dead room, Bob Oakland and the translator looked at each other, both certain their time together was drawing to an end. They wanted death, but not like this. Butchered in a secret complex in western Syria or northern Iraq. It was inhumane, a barbarism that shouldn't have been possible within the human race, and yet one that history had proven time and time again was prevalent. War crimes, genocides, torture, rape, mass exterminations, mutilations—people blamed them on monsters working the system. Bob now believed it didn't make sense. The world couldn't be awash with monsters who were waiting for the right opportunity to unleash their true potential. Instead, he now decided that the truth was much more unpalatable. We are all monsters. It's just that most people don't know it because their lives are okay, and they're never put in a situation where bloodlust couples with an insane survival instinct. If Bob were released from his ropes and chains, given a knife, and his wounds and strength allowed, he'd go crazy, be a savage beast, a monster and rip apart the jihadists and keep ripping them apart when they were dead. Perhaps Ramzi would be the same.

No.

As desperate as both men were, the image just didn't seem right. It was impossible for Ramzi and him to do stuff like that because there were no monsters lurking inside them. The thought gave him hope for humanity though he had no hope for his own civility because he was as good as dead.

The camera was placed on a tripod in the center of the room. One of the Chechens stood behind it, facing the red Arabic letters on the far wall. The chains locking Bob and Ramzi to the walls were released from their catches. Both men were dragged nearer to the camera and forced onto their knees. Five of the jihadists stood behind them, scarves wrapped around their faces. The camera was turned on.

In English, the unit's leader said, "Hello again, Mr. President. If you are a merciless pig who hates Americans, today will be these men's last day on Earth." He slapped Bob's head with sufficient force to cause blood to whip out of the CIA officer's mouth and fly across the room. "You shouldn't be surprised. We gave you fair warnings. It's just that so far you haven't listened."

Bob thought his ear might be perforated. The noise on that side of his head was severe though he could still hear the jihadist's words.

"This evening it will begin. You will watch what happens in our final video. But you have four hours to change the course of events. If Arzam Saud is released, and you can convince me that you have a plan that doesn't entail trying to kill us as we exchange prisoners, then I give you my word that these men will be kept alive and returned to you." He moved in front of Bob, crouched so that his face was at the same level as Bob's, and asked the CIA officer, "Would you like to go home?" He smiled; his eyes were cold. "I bet you would, you miserable dog."

Bob wanted to spit in his face, tell him to go fuck himself, and show as much defiance as was possible from a man who was bound in ropes. But things had now changed within him. He felt helpless and resigned to his plight. The man he'd been up to two days ago belonged to an unwanted story. Everything here was all too real. Too horrific. Too repulsive to be in a tale.

Bob looked directly into the camera. His bloodshot eyes were dried-up windows to a savaged soul; they had nothing to give anymore beyond telling the world that this could happen to anyone if they were unlucky. He murmured something, but it came out all wrong and was unintelligible. He glanced at Ramzi, who was staring at him, a look of utter desperation on the translator's face. Ramzi nodded. Bob didn't know why or what it meant. Maybe Ramzi was silently telling Bob that whatever he did or said, Ramzi would be shoulder to shoulder with the CIA officer and share whatever suffering came as a result.

Bob cleared his throat; he wanted to be stronger and wondered if in fact he and Ramzi had been extremely strong to make it this far.

He said, "Mr. President, I want to come home."

CHAPTER 21

One hour ago, Will had landed in Washington, D.C.'s Dulles International Airport. Via London, he'd flown business class from Moscow, purchasing a suit and toiletries at Heathrow and availing himself of the business-class departure lounge's facilities to shower, shave, change into his new clothes, and make himself look nothing like a man who'd recently killed someone in a park.

The journey from London to D.C. had been agonizingly long, not helped by the fact that he'd had to sit next to a loud-mouthed Silicon Valley entrepreneur who'd spent the whole journey bragging to Will about how many billions of dollars were sitting in his bank account. In fairness to the entrepreneur, his last words to Will were self-effacing and deferential. When the aircraft was taxiing toward the arrivals area of the airport, the captain had welcomed passengers to Washington and added that there would be a slight delay in disembarking because the plane was carrying a VIP who had to leave the craft first. The plane had stopped a hundred yards away from its allotted spaced; police cars with lights flashing had raced onto the concourse and stopped by the plane; and uniform cops and plainclothes Secret Service agents had entered the plane and told Will to come with them. As Will grabbed his luggage out of the overhead locker, the entrepreneur had said to him, "I've spent the whole flight talking about how great I am. But, who the fuck are you?"

Now Will was sitting in a straight-backed chair in the center of the Oval Office. The president was sitting behind his desk at one end of the room. Standing close to him were Chief of Staff Donny Tusk, head of the Joint Special Operations Command Lieutenant General Jerry Kinnear, and Will's former handler, CIA director Patrick Bolte. Moments ago, there'd been other politicians and senior military and intelligence personnel in the room, all here to watch the latest video of Bob Oakland. Tusk had ordered all of them to leave when Will had arrived.

Will was facing the four men, his legs crossed and his hands clasped. He was motionless, his brilliant intellect calculating hundreds of facts about the men before him. Only Patrick suspected the MI6 officer was mentally raping them, but he was reassured to note that Will betrayed no signs of doing so.

"We have sixty minutes left to release Saud and post a video on the Internet advising everyone that we've done so." The president looked at Kinnear. "Tell him."

The general addressed Will. "We've got Saud in a holding pen at McGuire AFB—McGuire military airbase in New Jersey. We video him getting on that plane. We tell the terrorists that we're flying him to the Middle East. When we've landed, we tell the terrorists to call our embassy in Baghdad.

Our ambassador will field that call in person. He'll ask for the grid reference where his captors want to make the exchange. We stick to our word. The exchange is clean. No military intervention."

"And in doing so, we get our boy back at the price of negotiating with terrorists." The president looked weary. "I can't let the world watch Bob and his aide be hacked to pieces. I'll be damned if I do. Trouble is, I'll be damned if I don't."

Will's eyes darted between each man before settling back on the president. "Don't make the trade."

Kinnear's fist thumped the president's desk. "You're playing with lives, son!"

"I never play. Don't make the trade."

Donny Tusk folded his arms while studying Will. "You think we shouldn't give in to terrorists' demands?"

"Of course, but my stance is underpinned by specifics. I don't believe they'll kill Oakland if we refuse to budge though I could be wrong." Will saw hostility on all of the men's faces, even in his loyal friend Patrick's expression. "I realize my advice carries with it some degree of risk."

"*Degree of risk?*" Kinnear stood, his face crimson. "You arrogant son of a bitch!"

Will was unflustered. "Arrogance is a sense of superiority over others, coupled with contempt for the weak. I have no such contempt. Nor do I think I'm superior to any living organism on this planet. But weakness is pertinent. Ramzi is weak. Even tough Bob Oakland looks like he's been broken. We are weak. We must all help each other. And the only way to do that is to stand firm."

Patrick's expression changed to one of concern as he

looked at Will. "If you've got this wrong, my friend, it'll be on your head. You're making an almighty call."

"Actually, it's *my* head and *my* call." The president asked Will, "Isn't that correct, Mr. Cochrane?"

Will replied, "You make decisions based upon the information supplied to you. If my information is shit, you have my complete permission to shoot the messenger."

"That's not how it happens, at least not around me." The president pointed a finger at Will. "Still, I'm not making a decision until I've heard everything. Why do you think we shouldn't give in to their demands?"

The men were silent as Will spoke for ten minutes.

"Jeez," said Tusk as he rubbed his face. He looked at the president. "But they still might kill Oakland and the translator anyway."

"The chief of staff's right." Will's eyes were unblinking as he stared at the president. "I'm certain what I've told you is fact. But I cannot predict what the terrorists will do if we face them down. They may kill Oakland simply out of spite or to tie up loose ends."

Kinnear, Tusk, and Bolte started arguing with each other, with the president listening carefully to each man's point of view.

"I have a solution."

The four men stopped talking and looked at the MI6 officer.

Will elaborated, "Mr. President: send them a video message. After it's finished, you will receive a call. I will give you the precise words to say to the caller." He wrote on a piece of paper. Tusk grabbed the paper and handed it to the president.

When the president finished reading the few lines, he sat in silence for a minute, deep in thought. He lifted his head and said to his chief of staff, "Get a camera and technicians in here. Now!"

The technicians wanted longer to test audio levels and lighting, but thanks to Tusk's threats to have them impaled on stakes if they didn't move faster, they were ready to shoot within three minutes of entering the room.

The president made his address to the camera. "We want proof of life. Get Bob Oakland to make a call to the White House. I must speak with him."

After the camera was turned off, and the technicians told to leave, the five men waited. All except Will kept glancing at their watches and wall clocks. In thirty minutes, Bob and Ramzi were going to be slowly executed on film.

Thirty minutes became twenty.

Kinnear started to sweat. "What if they haven't seen the video?"

Calmly, Will said, "They have. Monitoring the Internet is vital to them at this juncture."

Twenty became ten.

Then nine.

Then eight.

Donny Tusk was pacing. "Shit! Shit!"

Seven.

Kinnear was on the verge of panic when he exclaimed, "We get the camera back in here! Tell them we make the trade!"

Six.

Five.

The president's phone rang. One of his staff spoke to him and said he had a call that needed to be urgently transferred to the Oval Office. The president waited. He said, "Hello, Bob."

Bob Oakland's voice was thin. "Mr. President. Sir. It's me. I . . ."

Patrick wrote quickly on a piece of paper and shoved it in front of the president. The president read his instruction. "Bob: I've got to ask you a few questions. Ones that only you know the answers to. I need to check you are who you say you are. You okay with that?"

"Yes . . . yes."

The president spoke to Oakland for a minute, asking him about CIA protocols and codes that the president and Oakland were cleared to know. He looked at his staff and nodded.

It was the real Bob Oakland on the phone.

The president said, "Hang in there, Bob. You've got a whole bunch of people, me included, who think you're a hero to have survived what you've gone through. When we get you out of this situation, I'm going to meet you in person and make sure the world knows the remarkable service you've done for our country. But we've got matters to attend to first. Put their leader on. I need to say something to him." The line went quiet.

The Chechen jihadist spoke. "You have less than two minutes. After that, I must hang up and set to work on your fellow American."

The president picked up the paper Will had given him, and word for word relayed its contents. "We know everything about Arzam Saud. You want the world to know that Saud is a terrorist. Now, so do I. I'm not doing a public trade with you. That would undermine my position. But, it would also undermine yours. Trust issues would come into play. Was Saud brainwashed by us and turned when he was in captivity? Is he going to report back to us about ISIS? Islamic State won't fully trust him. Maybe they won't trust him at all. His stock could hit rock bottom. But I see your plight, and I'm very sympathetic to it. Though I don't agree with what you've done, we share the same values and concerns. It's in my interest to see matters are put right. One day soon, Arzam Saud will escape. We'll make sure of that. He'll make his way back to you. Probably he'll rough up a few people along the way. That'll look good. He'll be hailed a hero by ISIS. His stock will hit the roof. He can go back to being a terrorist. In return, I ask that there is no more blood and that hearts remain beating. Do I have your agreement?"

There was silence at the end of the phone.

Then, the line went dead.

CHAPTER 22

Bob's eyes opened. Had he been asleep? Knocked unconscious? Or was this how it worked when you reached the other side?

He just lay on the ground for a while, breathing, trying to work out what was happening while wondering if all this was real or a dream. The room looked like the same one he'd been in since he'd been captured. But three things were different. The red words were no longer on the wall. All of his shackles had been removed. And Ramzi was nowhere to be seen.

Was this a trick?

Probably.

Soon, he'd be back in chains, on his knees, jihadists laughing as they sawed through his gullet.

Still, it was nice to think otherwise. Even if it was a foolish thought.

And it was nice of the president to try to reassure him, and tell him he'd give him medals, and would announce to the world that Oakland was the finest son of America. It was like a parent trying to comfort his child at the end of the phone, the parent not knowing where the child is, the child being trapped in a coffin, deep underground somewhere no one could find him.

That cool breeze? Where was it coming from? It felt so good on his painful skin. A draft, he guessed. A change of wind direction, perhaps. He'd never felt the breeze in here before.

Bob forced himself to his feet, yelping in pain from the rope injuries on his legs. He staggered forward, calling out in a hushed voice, "Ramzi? Ramzi! What's going on?"

Maybe Ramzi couldn't answer because he was being torn apart in the room next door.

He reached the wall where Ramzi had been tethered, next to the red letters that had faced Oakland for every second of his incarceration.

Dead Room.

He touched the area where the letters had been. It was damp. They'd been washed off very recently. Oakland wondered if the trick they were playing on him was to make him think he'd lost his mind. They needn't have bothered. If he had any sanity left, it was so wafer thin that the cool breeze he felt was liable to make it snap. "Ramzi—are you dead?" he asked as he limped to the door. Ramzi didn't answer. Bob placed his hand on the door handle, deciding that they'd slaughtered Ramzi and left Bob trapped in here with no food and water so that he could surely go insane and die.

He turned the handle.

The door opened.

The breeze was refreshing though Oakland ignored it because his heart was beating fast with fear and hope. He wished he didn't have the hope. It was so cruel. So tantalizing. So utterly fucking futile.

"Ramzi—did they murder you? Bury you in the desert? Eat you? Piss on you? Tell me, please. I need to know. It'll help me prepare myself for what they'll do to me. Please, Ramzi."

He looked in the adjacent room. No hangman's rope; the bench was gone.

"They ate you, Ramzi." Bob staggered onward along a corridor. "My poor Ramzi. Disappeared forever."

He passed other rooms, all of them empty, and reached the end of the corridor. He opened the door and walked into what looked like a warehouse. There were piles of metal girders, rusty machinery, conveyor belts covered in dust and mildew, and a tractor and trailer that was on bricks and had no wheels. The vehicle looked like it had been stripped of every spare part that might be useful. No, this wasn't a warehouse. A long time ago, it had been a factory.

At its far end was an open door, and beyond it, brilliant white light.

"Heaven or Hell," Oakland muttered between gritted teeth. "I don't care. Either's better than this place." He limped onward. "You out there, Ramzi? What's it like? Harps and grapes, or goats with forks?"

Maybe Ramzi was now an angel, waiting for him in the white light, his huge wings outstretched, a smile on his face as he hovered above the ground. He hoped so. It would be sad if instead he confronted his translator in a barrel of boiling tar, burning alive for eternity.

The breeze was stronger. His eyes were squinting because the light was so damn fierce. God's light? The devil's light?

Either or, it hurt. Mustn't look directly at God, he reminded himself. It's rude to do so. Be polite. Say sorry for the naughty things you've done. Move along.

He reached the door and stopped, his heart still beating fast, his mouth open.

What he saw looked like the outskirts of a town or large village. A road was here. So, too, houses, telegraph poles carrying cables, and banks of grass that ran alongside the road's edge. The place looked poor but not impoverished—more like the blue-collar working towns that Bob had grown up in. It appeared deserted. The sky was blue, the temperature pleasant. The breeze continued to wash over him as he staggered down the center of the road.

"Hello! Anyone here?"

Maybe this was a Syrian village whose occupants had been gassed to death. A ghost town remained. Yes, that's what happened. It had been decided by higher powers that Bob Oakland had been condemned to an everlasting existence within a chemical attack. That sucked.

There was movement farther down the road. Something black. Bob couldn't decide if it was an imp, demon, or creepy ghost girl. It had legs and arms, for sure. Don't trust it, Bob told himself. It might play at being nice, but it wants your liver and kidneys.

The black creature grew nearer. Walking. Not a ghost girl, instead an old witch. She had a headscarf on, her back was bent, and a stick was in one hand. Of course, her frailty was all bogus. Don't eat anything she offers you. It'll be laced with poison. Pretend you don't know what she really is. Maybe she'll leave you alone.

The old woman got very close and stopped, her expression quizzical. She shrieked while holding her mouth to her hand and staring at the walking corpse that Bob resembled. "Peter! Peter!" she cried out while looking at a house across the street.

A middle-aged man in overalls ran out of the house and came to Bob's side. He placed a hand on Bob's shoulder, concern and confusion all over his face. "What happened?" he asked in a language that wasn't English or Arabic.

But Bob understood and spoke the language very well. The man's question hade made Bob's thinking sharpen and his sanity return. And it made him realize that he'd been victim to the biggest trick of all. "Where am I?" he croaked.

The woman asked, "What happened to you? Were you in an accident? Robbed?" She glanced at Peter, then back at Oakland. "My son will get you help. We have a car. We'll take you to a hospital."

"Where am I?" Bob repeated.

It was Peter who answered. "Our town is ten miles south of St. Petersburg. You're in Russia."

CHAPTER 23

The president, Tusk, Kinnear, Bolte, and Will Cochrane were still in the Oval Office.

Will remained sitting on the chair in the center of the room, his eyes closed and his fingertips pressed against each other. His mind was no longer occupied with thinking; instead, it was poised to pounce on breaking developments. And he was oblivious to the others in the room. Right now, anything they said, did, or conjectured on was irrelevant. All that mattered was what could happen outside the room. Only when news of that event reached the confines of the Oval Office would Will open his eyes and engage his brain.

The president's phone rang.

His chief of staff picked it up, listened, and hung up.

Will opened his eyes and looked at Tusk.

Tusk broke out into an uncharacteristic beam. "We've got him! Our consulate in St. Petersburg. He was taken there by a couple of Russians. Oakland's on U.S. diplomatic soil now, and we're flying him home. He's in bad shape, but he's being patched up and will be fine."

Patrick winked at Will. "And he'll have some big stories to tell when he gets home."

The president momentarily closed his eyes and slowly exhaled. He nodded, and looked at Will. "Sir, I'm in your debt. Whatever your price, you name it."

Will got to his feet, approached the most powerful man in the world, withdrew a slip of paper, and placed it in front of the president. "My price."

The president frowned. "What's this?"

"Parking ticket. Seventy-five pounds. It's a lot of money. The bastards got me in south London's Oswin Street. I'm not sure if you have any influence over the Southwark Council?"

Exasperated, Patrick grabbed the ticket. "Tell you what—let's let the CIA go head to head with your local council and see who comes out on top." He laughed and held out his hand. "Well done!"

Will shook his hand, a slight smile on his face.

Kinnear stood before the MI6 officer. "Unconventional thinking seems to have paid off." For once, his hostility was absent when he added, "And thank goodness for that. But it was an almighty problem for you to solve."

It had been one of Will Cochrane's most challenging cases.

Arzam Saud was not a terrorist though he had been made to look like one by Russia. Saud was a Russian asset, recruited by a Russian intelligence officer who was previously a KGB operative until he worked for its successor, the SVR. That officer had assumed the false name of Viktor Gorsky. Gorsky had been operating undercover as a businessman with that name ever since he had killed the real Gorsky in Afghanistan.

Since then, Gorsky ran a high-ranking front for funneling SVR money and paying its assets. In order to hide his role, the KGB and its successor SVR set up the banks Trans Forex and Moscow Vision for the sole purpose of being the legitimate funding vehicles of another Russian intelligence front—the company KapSet. Gorsky was the pivotal public face of these institutions and was essential to use Russian money to entrap potential foreign assets. Saud was one such asset. His age and nationality were deemed ideal for someone who might become a fundamentalist. His intellect was also important. The SVR needed a thinking spy, not a mindless crazy.

Gorsky got to him in two ways. First, he lured him into partnering on property deals. Second, he got him taking Russian sweetener bribes. Then Gorsky told Saud who he really was. By then, Saud was in too deep to have a way out. Gorsky had his hooks in him and forced him to work for the Russians.

Saud was used to penetrate ISIS and was a key source of intelligence to Russia. But he got caught by pro-Yazidis, who handed him over to the Americans, believing him to be a bona fide ISIS soldier. Russia constructed a plot to pose as ISIS wannabes, capture a CIA officer, use him as leverage, and get their prized asset Saud released.

The translator Ramzi was the one who had tipped the Russians off about the CIA officer's meeting with Shiite elders. He, too, was on Gorsky's payroll.

The six alleged ISIS Chechen Muslims were in fact cadre Russian SVR operatives acting the part. They wanted the West to be terrified for the fate of the CIA officer. Pretending to be ISIS wannabes would do that.

But Will had gotten to the truth and given the president words that would not only call the Russians' bluff but also tell them that America and Russia shared the same enemy and purpose. When the president had spoken to the leader of the six-man unit, he'd used subtle language to tell the man that he knew Saud worked for Russia and was vital to the war against ISIS. But he also hinted that trading Saud for Oakland could backfire against the interests of both Russia and America. The better solution would be for Russia to walk away from Oakland and for Saud to escape U.S. custody at some point in the near future. Russia would reactivate Saud, and he'd be sent back to ISIS, where he'd be hailed as a returning hero by the jihadists and continue to spy on them on behalf of Russia.

Russia's tactics had been brutal. With Ramzi's permission, they'd even had to torture the translator in order to fool Oakland and others that he was a victim. Now, Ramzi remained on the payroll of SVR and its legitimate face in the person of Gorsky. The translator had played the part well.

The president shook his head. "Russia tried to put one over on us. Thanks to you, they failed though it still feels like I've done a deal with the devil."

Will was about to leave but hesitated, pondering the president's observation. "Russia wants ISIS obliterated as much as we do. That's why it did everything it could to get Saud released. It wasn't a deal with the devil, sir. Rather, it was a deal with a state whose interests have momentarily overlapped with our own. What makes you uncomfortable is Russia's methods. Perhaps"—he smiled—"it would be in order to remind Russia that we don't need to play such games." He wrote on a scrap of paper. To the president, he said, "On the day before we allow Arzam Saud to escape back to his Russian masters, give him this and tell him to give it to Viktor Gorsky."

Will turned and walked out of the room. He knew what would happen next. Still, one had to try to make the world and the people within in it aspire to the greater good.

The president read Will's words.

> *Dead Russian philosopher Nikolai Berdyaev said, There is a tragic clash between truth and the world; pure undistorted truth burns up the world. Berdyaev would be turning in his grave if he could see how wrong his observation now is. We, and you, are burning up the world with distorted truth. This, and the fact you are looking at the man holding this paper, is a reminder to you that it needn't be thus.*

The president folded the paper into neat squares. "Russia's not the only one that has those kinds of methods." He smiled and tore the paper into pieces.

ACKNOWLEDGMENTS

With thanks to David Highfill and Luigi Bonomi and their brilliant teams at William Morrow and LBA, respectively; Judith; and my eleven- and twelve-year-old children who ask me profound questions about the "grown-up" world that I strive to cryptically answer in my books.

Keep reading for an excerpt from

THE SPY HOUSE,

the next installment in
Matthew Dunn's thrilling
Spycatcher series

Coming in hardcover October 2015

CHAPTER 1

Place des Vosges, Paris

Israel's ambassador to France was due to retire in three months, but that wasn't going to happen because in six minutes, he'd be dead.

He had no inkling of his imminent demise, as he was a healthy fifty-nine-year-old who'd recently undergone a full medical checkup and had told by his doctor that he wasn't going to die anytime soon. In fairness, his doctor could not be expected to anticipate that his patient's heart might be targeted by a sniper.

The ambassador was not alone as he walked through Paris's oldest square. Tourists were ambling nearby, taking photos of the striking and identical seventeenth-century red-brick houses that surrounded the square. Children were playing tag, running through the vaulted arcades. Lovers were strolling arm in arm, admiring the manicured lawns that partly covered the interior of the square and the rows of trees that had turned an autumnal russet.

Walking forty yards behind the ambassador were three men who had pistols secreted under their suit jackets.

The ambassador took a walk through the square every lunchtime, and on each occasion his bodyguards wished they could be closer to their charge. But the ambassador was stubborn and insisted they keep their distance so that he could have space to unclutter his mind from the hundreds of tasks and problems sent his way during the course of the morning.

Today, he was deep in thought on one issue: indications that American and European support for Israel was on the wane.

He reached the fountain in the center of the square and stopped. He'd been here so many times that his eyes barely registered his surroundings nor his ears the sound of running water. His bodyguard detail also stopped, silently wishing the ambassador wouldn't do things like this and make him an easy target. Their hands were close to their weapons, ready to pull them out and shoot anyone who ran toward the senior diplomat while carrying a knife, bomb, or gun.

The ambassador moved on.

His protectors kept pace with him.

They were good bodyguards—ex–Special Forces who'd been given subsequent training in surveillance, close protection, evasive driving, and rapid takedown of hostile attackers. But the Place des Vosges was a nightmare environment for such men. Too big, too many buildings, windows, people, entrances and exits, and open spaces. They couldn't be blamed for not spotting the sniper behind one of the top-floor windows of a house that was seventy yards away. That window was one of hundreds that looked onto the square. And the sniper had chosen it because at this time of day the sun reflected off it and made it impossible to see anyone behind the glass.

There was no noise when the bullet left his silenced rifle, penetrated the window, traveled across the square, and entered the ambassador's heart. But when the diplomat collapsed to the ground, the square became chaotic and loud. Some people were running toward the dead man shouting. Others screamed, remained still, held hands to their mouths and pointed at the body. The bodyguards raced to the ambassador, yelling at everyone to get out of their way, their withdrawn handguns now inducing fear and panic in those in the square.

Many believed the armed men must have shot the man. Some fled the scene; others threw themselves to the ground; mothers grabbed their children and held them close, their expressions filled with horror. The bodyguards ignored them all.

When they reached the body, they rolled it onto its back. They cursed in Hebrew as they saw the bullet entry point in the ambassador's chest. One of them checked for a pulse though it was obvious the diplomat was dead. The others scoured their surroundings for signs of a man holding a high-velocity rifle.

They saw no one like that.

The sniper had vanished.

CHAPTER 2

The Palestinian boy Safa was thirteen years old though he had the head of an older teenager because he'd grown up too fast in Gaza. That had happened because of Israeli artillery shells, everyone he knew being in abject poverty, the constant stench of decay in Gaza's northern city of Jabalia, and having to worry all of his life about where the next morsel of food and drop of liquid might come from. But underneath his smooth, golden skin, black hair, and blue eyes, he was still a child—one who was encouraged by his parents to read nineteenth-century adventure stories, had a penchant for making model Jewish soldiers and Arab freedom fighters out of bits of broken wood from shacks and scraps of cloth taken from the dead, and drawing paintings that most often contained an imaginary mighty blue river coursing through the center of Gaza, people drinking from it and bathing and smiling at each other because it was a God-given source of life and hope. Though he was wiser than his years, he was, other Jabalia residents lamented, a dreamer. They worried about him.

Especially those who resided in the large refugee camp,

where he survived alongside his dying mom and dad, a place that was cramped with the hopeless, forgotten by all but Western do-gooders and Israeli undercover soldiers. Here there were tents that were torn and laced with bacteria, decrepit huts that afforded no protection from wind and rats, once fine-looking buildings that were now bombed-out shells, and oil barrels that were torn in half and littered along dusty tracks, some containing burning rags, others brewing insipid broth that was being stirred by women and watched over with eager anticipation by lines of starving people.

Approximately one hundred thousand refugees lived in the camp. Rarely did any of them smile. But not all were like that. There was humor to be found in the camp, and Safa witnessed it as he ran along an alley toward his home.

"Hey, Safa," called out Jasem, a thirty-nine-year-old seller of anything, a career he'd taken up after realizing his previous vocation of creating tunnels into Israel was unsustainable because of his claustrophobia, "what you running for? Nobody here has anything to run to."

Safa grinned. "I'm keeping fit."

"Me too." Jasem started doing squats, his expression mimicking the exertions of an Olympic weight lifter. "I'm on a high-protein diet. It feeds the muscles."

Safa ran on, his skinny limbs hurting from malnutrition, his hand clutching a white piece of paper.

"Go, Safa. Go, Safa," chanted two young Arab girls, clapping in time with each word. They were smiling though some of their teeth were missing.

One of them asked, "Are you playing, Pretend the Israeli Soldier's Chasing Me?"

"I have a piece of paper," Safa replied, racing onward.

Safa reached his home—a room in a crumbling building that had decades ago been the residence of a benign judge and his wealthy family. People like his parents. All of the building's other rooms were three-sided, thanks to Israeli shells that had destroyed their outer walls; only this room was intact. But it was a small room and smelled bad. These days, his father spent most of his life on the rotting mattress in the corner of the room. His mother tried her best to wash their sheets as regularly as she could, but water was scant, and her strength was failing. Safa's bed was piled-up blankets in another corner of the room. They were crawling with bugs and exuded a scent of overripe cheese. And in the center of the room was a clay pot that cooked everything they ate. Mealtimes, when they could be had, were taken sitting on the floor. To do so hurt his mother's increasingly skin-and-bones physique, but she insisted on the ritual for the sake of Safa. He had to be taught good manners, she had told him many times, and learn that a meal eaten properly is a meal well deserved. His father, however, could now only be spoon-fed by his mom while he was lying on his back. It broke her heart to see him like this.

"Mama," Safa said, breathing deeply to catch his breath, "I have a piece of paper!"

"Good." His mother tried to smile though she was exhausted. "The Israelis are starving Gaza to death, yet you have a piece of paper. Today is a good day."

She was by her husband, mopping his brow with a rag. His eyes were closed, and he moaned quietly.

"It could be a good day." Safa thrust the paper at arm's

length in front of him. "A man from the United Nations says he can help me. The UN, he told me, can get me to France, where I can be given food, an education, and maybe even asylum."

Safa's mom got awkwardly to her feet, wincing as she did so. She took the paper and read it. The words were in French, but that didn't matter because everyone in her family spoke and read French like natives of the tongue. "A consent form?"

"Yes, Mama. It needs your signature."

"Where did you meet this man?"

"At school. He'd brought books and stationery to my teacher. He asked her which of her pupils showed most academic promise." Safa's face beamed. "She told him, me."

"And how would he get you out of here, to France?"

"My teacher asked him the same question. She then told me to wait on the other side of the classroom while she spoke to the man. They were speaking for a long time. Me and the rest of my friends couldn't hear what they were saying. Then my teacher called me over. She put her arms on me and said that this was a great opportunity to have a new life."

Had this conversation been held two years ago, his mother might have had the strength to shed a tear and been utterly conflicted as to what to do. But the death of Safa's younger sister from an undiagnosed disease and of her and her husband's rapid decline in health made her emotions numb and her decision inevitable. She knew Safa's father would pass away at any time. His eyes were jaundiced, his skin color ashen—almost certainly he had lung disease; and if that didn't kill him, then the fact that his body could no longer absorb nutrients would. She, too, was not long for this world. The once-beautiful woman had caught a glimpse of her image in a broken glass window the other day. She was horrified to see how she now looked. So thin, her face etched and drawn, nothing at all like the pretty girl who'd daily brushed her long shiny hair in front of a vanity mirror. She'd tried to do everything she could for Safa. But even if she were fully fit, she'd be running out of options. There was nothing left in Gaza. It was a country that was being strangled to death.

She sighed as she reread the paper. "The United Nations man must be breaking rules."

"That's what my teacher told me. She said I wasn't to care and should have no fear. She said he was a good man. Would find me a good home. Would give me a new life."

His mother went to her son and hugged him. "My Safa. Is this what you want?"

Safa looked at his mom's face, and tears ran down his face. "I don't know, Mama. I *am* scared."

This was her final act of strength. The last opportunity for her to save at least one member of her family. She pointed north. "Over the border are people whose grandparents faced these kinds of situations when they were your age. They came from Russia, Germany, France, other places. They didn't know what lay ahead. But they knew what lay behind. They had no choice." She didn't add that, as a result, their sons and grandsons should have known better than to do what they were doing to this small strip of land and its population. "But it worked out well for them. They became scholars, businessmen, soldiers, had families, and now they have smiles on their faces and bellies that are full. You must go."

Safa's voice was wavering as he asked, "What if he's a bad man?"

His mother stroked a frail finger against her son's hair. "My experience of people in the United Nations is that they can be naïve but never bad. But if this man turns out to be bad, you run." She smiled. "And even that won't be so bad because you'll be running in a land of fat bellies." She managed to smile. "When everything else is stripped away, it all comes down to food and water. But only you can decide what to do."

Safa went to his father's side. "Papa, Papa? What should I do? Must I leave you?"

His father looked at him, resignation and illness so evident. "*We* must leave *you*, my dear boy."

"But, Papa . . ."

"You have no choice."

Safa placed his head on his father's chest. "How could they do this to you, to us, to everyone here?"

His father stroked his son's hair. "They didn't do something. Our neighboring country did nothing. There is a difference."

"It still makes them bad."

His father's voice was soothing as he replied, "No, no. If that were true, then we would all be bad. Charities we ignore, famines elsewhere in the world, disasters, wars, abuse—we can't solve them all. Does that make us murderers? I think not."

Safa wept. "The Israelis starve us."

"And some of us hurt them back. Evil lurks on both sides of the borders. But it isn't and cannot be pervasive."

Safa held his hand, it was limp and felt wrong. "Mama—Papa isn't moving."

His mother nodded, resignation flowing over her, a feeling that death had exited one body and was drifting across the room to devour her. She had no need to move to her son's side. This moment had been coming for so long. It was inevitable. There was no heartache; that had happened ages ago. Since then it had just been about managing the situation, and logistics, including disposing of the body in a way that didn't add to the already disease-ridden melting pot of the Jabalia refugee camp. Burning corpses was usually the only way. Even then, one couldn't be sure that airborne bacteria and viruses wouldn't flee charred flesh and attack any nearby mourners.

"He has told you what you should do," was all she could say. She grabbed a pencil and put her signature on the bottom of the paper. "When do you go?"

"Tomorrow. I must meet him at the school. My teacher also needs to sign some forms. He will then take me to a boat. He told me to pack light."

"Pack? You have nothing to pack."

Safa went back to his mother and cuddled her. "Mama, please cook me stewed beef and garbanzo beans tonight."

His mother didn't have food. Couldn't. "We can pretend, okay?"

"Sure, Mama." He held her. "That will be delicious." His tears were unstoppable. "Delicious, Mama."

CHAPTER 3

Soil clung to the CIA officer's perspiring skin after he inadvertently rubbed the back of his aching hand against his forehead. Roger Koenig's sweat made some of the grime enter his eyes, and he had to blink fast to clear them. He grabbed his pickax, swung it over his head, and slammed it into the ground. Three other men were close to him, all natives of Iran's southwestern city of Shiraz, whose outskirts were ten miles north of their current location. They, too, were using shovels and pickaxes to dig, lanterns around the hole being the sole source of light in the pitch-dark night. Their grunts and the noise of their tools striking earth were the only sounds they could hear in the featureless and deserted rural location.

Reza was the twenty-nine-year-old son of a watchmaker who was by his side. He said, "I've hit something."

They all immediately stopped digging.

Roger lay flat on his stomach and placed his hand in the hole, which was seven feet long, four feet wide, and three feet deep. The CIA officer had to stretch to touch the bottom. There was no doubt Reza was right. They'd reached something that was metal. Thank God. Roger had previously shuddered at the idea they might find rotting mahogany that would reveal what was inside if they tried to remove the item. He didn't want that image in his head. It would be wrong.

Roger got to his feet and looked at the watchmaker. "Masoud. Very carefully."

Masoud nodded and placed a hand on his other son, "Firouz will clear the surface. We'll excavate around the box."

They got back to work, this time making smaller indentations with their tools so as not to inadvertently damage the box. It took them nearly an hour to uncover it completely and allow enough space for them to stand next to the container. One man at each corner, they slowly lifted the heavy box that was as long as Roger was tall, and placed it next to the hole.

Breathing fast, Roger grabbed a rag and wiped his face and hands. "Okay. Let's move. Box in the truck first. Then all equipment."

Masoud asked, "Do we refill the hole?"

"No time for that."

They drove nearly four hundred kilometers through the night, Reza at the wheel and where possible his foot to the floor because they were all desperate to reach the southern port of Bandar-e 'Abbâs before daybreak. They made it with one hour to spare, Reza avoiding the main roads as he expertly navigated his way through the medium-sized city until they reached the shores of the Persian Gulf. Boats of all shapes and sizes were moored alongside jetties and harbor walls. Most of them were motorized cargo vessels, some were powerful speedboats. All of them were the type of craft that would have gotten them away from Iran and its naval patrols in quick time. But they were too obvious. Instead, Roger had decided they needed to escape in something that no fugitives in their right minds would use.

That vessel was now in front of them. A traditional dhow that had one big white sail but no motor.

Reza parked the truck. "Fast, fast." He stayed in the vehicle as the other men ran to the back of the truck, grabbed the metal container, and carried it quickly along a jetty and onto the boat. Reza was driving away as they lowered the box onto the deck. His destination was Shiraz where he'd put the truck in a secure garage and leave it locked in there until he was sure that it wasn't being looked for by Iranian police or the country's more insidious security agencies.

Roger was a former member of SEAL Team 6 who had proficiency with most types of seafaring vessels. That experience enabled him to help Masoud and Firouz prepare the dhow to sail. It took them only two minutes to get the vessel moving. Roger was of no use now aside from scouring their surroundings as his Iranian assets steered the vessel and made adjustments to its rigging. He did so for one hour as they crossed the Strait of Hormuz, and even as they exited Iranian waters unchallenged, he continued his vigil as they approached the United Arab Emirates and followed its shores until they entered Dubai's creek.

The CIA officer only let himself relax when they reached the inner part of the creek, where the majority of boats docked and unloaded their cargos.

The early-morning sun and balmy air soothed his weary face; there were noises of birds and men and vessels, but they were quiet, as if the creatures were half-asleep and respectful that others nearby were still in deep slumber. Roger wondered when he'd next sleep. Not for a while, he concluded.

He placed a hand on the metal box. It had taken him three years to identify its location, and he'd done so using his own money during downtime, when he wasn't deployed by the CIA, and sometimes vacation time, when he should have been with his family. He'd sacrificed a lot to locate and extract the container by tasking his Iranian sources, bribing officials, analyzing old CIA reports, talking to former Iranian intelligence officers turned CIA assets, and by putting his boots on Iranian ground and making his own inquiries. Many times he could have been captured and killed if anyone had established his objective. And if that had happened, the CIA would have rightly disavowed him because it, too, had no idea what he was doing.

His biggest fear now was that the thing in the box was not what he thought it was. After he took it to the American consulate in Dubai and it was flown back to the States, tests would be done on its contents. Then he'd find out if his efforts now and during the preceding years had been worth the sacrifice.

He dearly hoped so.

Because the box was his gift to a British MI6 officer who'd saved his life countless times.

A man who deserved some peace of mind in his otherwise mangled life.

A comrade.

A true friend called Will Cochrane.

CHAPTER 4

For the last few months, Britain's MI6 and its American equivalent, the CIA, believed that I'd been sitting at home doing nothing. MI6 occasionally checked up on me, but it had always given me advance notice of its visits, meaning I could make sure I was at my South London pad when the service's Welfare Department came knocking. Tonight, the agencies probably thought I was going out for a few beers to drown my sorrows. After all, tomorrow was officially my last day as an employed field operative of Western Intelligence because during my last mission, a malevolent U.S. senator revealed my identity to the world's media, I tore apart Washington, D.C., to get answers, and the joint U.S.-U.K. task force I worked for was shut down.

My employers told me I'd become a loose cannon without portfolio and added that I should be grateful that they were giving me four months on full pay to allow me to idle and decompress after nine years of near-constant deployment. And I was told to use that time to learn how to integrate into normal society. Trouble was, I don't do decompression or integration well, and though I've enough sorrows to fill up a hundred lives, I rarely feel the need to drown them.

Instead, they are prone to drowning me if I stay still for too long.

So, I'd been busy. Secretly busy.

Traveling to different parts of the world; obtaining weapons, and other equipment, and secreting them in dead-letter boxes within the major cities; meeting my foreign assets and telling them that one day I might still have a use for them; and tying up loose ends. Only two people knew what I'd been up to: my former bosses Alistair McCulloch and Patrick Bolte from MI6 and the CIA, respectively. They'd helped me where they could with cash, and information, and covered my ass when needed. But even they didn't know that tonight I wasn't propping up a bar in London and instead was in Hong Kong, walking through the Temple Street Night Market.

It was a tying-up-loose-ends evening.

I was observing a Chinese woman who's a highly prized intelligence operative who'd spent her entire career combating the West. I was behind her, disguised as a seaman onshore for a night out after twelve months on a tanker. She was unaware of me and the threat I posed. Around us were hundreds of tourists and locals, haggling with the multitude of vendors who'd crammed central Kowloon's most popular bazaar with stalls selling counterfeit goods, clothes, noodles, and still-twitching bottom-feeding sea life. People were shouting, calling out to each other, opera was being sung by troupes busking for a few dollars outside stinking public toilets, and junkies were arguing with old men as they faced each other over games of Chinese chess. Few people would hear a woman scream in pain if someone killed her on the street, and no one would care if they heard such a noise. There was too much sensory overload to notice anything odd in this bustling and bruising place: people banging into each other; a heavy rain descending from the late-summer night sky; vast banners with Cantonese characters overhanging the street and flapping loudly in the wind; glowing Chinese lanterns suspended in the air; the smell of crustaceans, soy sauce, and burning incense; and swathes of dazzling neon light around each stall.

But there were also big chunks of darkness on the street, and that was where most people moved, their eyes transfixed by the areas of brilliant glow, like flies that were attracted to illuminated and electrified death traps.

Street-canny prostitutes chose to work the low-rise tenements behind the stalls. This was a place where they could do their business and men could come and pay them and go without being noticed.

It was also an excellent place to visit death on unwitting victims.

I increased speed as the woman picked up her pace, then stopped as my target perused a stall containing fake silks that were cotton and powdered rhino horn that was actually a lethal combination of ground stone, fiberglass, and bamboo root. I watched the target to see if this was a deliberate stop to catch sight of me.

Woman moved; I moved.

I had a knife on me. It was the best weapon for tonight because my target would be taking no chances and would almost certainly be carrying a silenced pistol or blade.

We were getting close to my kill zone.

The woman checked her watch, gave a physical gesture of annoyance, and turned toward me.

Shit!

I was a mere ten feet away from her, alongside lots of men, women, kids, and crackheads. Maybe if the woman looked at me, she'd think I had a bloodlust. I didn't. I had a job to do, and right now it was one that would take the woman completely by surprise.

But she didn't spot me amid the throngs of people ahead of her. She was preoccupied, had clearly lost track of time, and used her cell phone to call her husband. Her partner took the brunt of her annoyance as she instructed him to get his car started and pick her up in five minutes or she'd stick something sharp in his gullet.

That wasn't going to happen.

Not if another man had his way.

For he wanted to stick his knife into her gullet.

And I was here to stop him dead.

My target walked fast toward the woman, his blade exposed. I rushed at the large Chinese man, grabbed his chin from behind, and plunged my blade into his throat. As he slumped to the ground, the Chinese woman's shock was amplified when she saw my face.

I walked past her, muttering, "Your cover's blown. Get out of China. Time to retire to somewhere safe."

The Chinese intelligence officer knew me well. Years ago, I'd turned her into an MI6 asset so that she could spy on her countrymen. Recently, I'd learned that her colleagues had discovered her treachery and tonight were deploying one of their best assassins to punish her. No way was I going to let that happen to such a courageous woman.

She opened her mouth to speak to me.

I didn't stop and, within seconds, had vanished into the night.

And in ninety minutes I'd use an alias passport to fly back to London.

No one would know that tonight an English killer had been in China and that his real name was Will Cochrane.

The reason Admiral Tobias Mason no longer wore a naval uniform was because five years ago, he'd reached a stage in his career where he'd felt embarrassed by how he looked. He'd spent thirty-four years on water, half of them captaining U.S. warships of mass destruction and frequently being the ultimate power in several thousand square miles of ocean. The problem with this was it gave him too many medals on his uniform. While inspecting his massed naval ranks on a sunny parade ground five years ago, the medals made him think he looked like a throwback military dictator.

Mason hated the idea of looking like a dictator because he was by nature a nonconformist individual who didn't like uniforms. In many ways he was the antithesis of a military man; the only reason he'd run away to sea as an adolescent was because his brain craved adventure. Nevertheless, his superiors in the navy quickly recognized his superb intellect and passion for unconventional tactics. They promoted him and kept telling him that one day he'd be an admiral. Mason didn't like the flattery because he could never jettison his nonconformist mind-set, and nor did he wish to. His idol was the nineteenth-century British admiral Lord Thomas Cochrane, a man who'd been a maverick throughout his career yet could conjure naval strategies that were brilliant and often improvised. Cochrane tore the rulebook up and won. But he was still made to dress like a clown.

Three years ago, the navy had asked Mason if he'd like a job on dry land that didn't require him to wear a uniform.

As he took a seat at the long rectangular conference table in the subterranean White House Situation Room, the diminutive silver-haired admiral wondered not for the first time whether he'd made the right decision to leave the sea. Dry land sometimes felt like it had too many captains trying to sail the same ship. It seemed that way now as America's political elite took seats around the table. They all knew Mason though none of them really understood what he did for a living. Given he was by nature a private man, it pleased him they didn't know he'd been singled out by the president for a very discreet role that required him to be the president's confidant and to think through solutions that were beyond the intellectual capabilities of the president's other advisors. It was a role that on paper didn't exist.

The president walked into the room and sat at the head of the table. His chief of staff was close behind him and turned on three wall-mounted TV monitors. Each screen showed a video link to the prime ministers of Britain, France, and Israel.

After formal introductions and greetings were exchanged, the Israeli prime minister dominated the first fifteen minutes of the meeting. He told everyone that a week ago, a senior

Hamas official had been killed by an Israeli missile strike in Gaza. Nobody in the room seemed particularly interested because Israel had made public the strike and kill, hours after it had happened. But as the Israeli prime minister moved on to the reason why this meeting had been called at such short notice, he made no attempt to hide his anger. His voice shook as he spoke about yesterday's assassination of Israel's ambassador to France. He spoke about how they'd gone to school together, served in the army as young men, attended each other's weddings, and on more than one occasion shared a drink while watching the sun go down over Tel Aviv.

Mason wasn't watching him. Instead, he was observing his American colleagues and the prime ministers of France and Britain. Did any of them know why they were here? Even the U.S. president hadn't been given a clear agenda for the meeting by the Israeli prime minister, beyond being told that it was to discuss what had happened in Paris. But Mason was sure he knew where this was headed.

He checked his watch and estimated that the Israeli would drop that bombshell in three minutes. In fact, he was fifteen seconds wide of the mark. And that was when the room became a chaotic cacophony of people trying to talk over each other, some trying to do so with insincere smiles on their faces, others looking hostile and slapping their hands on the table. During the following hour, the chief of staff had to call for order seven times. The room seemed evenly split between those who were for Israel's bombshell and those who were against. Mason was the only person who was silent throughout this unproductive period of too many generals and chiefs and secretaries of this and that all trying to take control of the ship and drive it in the wrong direction. He wanted to sigh but maintained his composed and professional demeanor while his mind raced.

The chief of staff called for order again, and this time he did so with the look of a man who'd rip anyone's head of if they didn't comply.

The president began asking people individually for not only their calm assessment but also whether there was a solution to this problem. All of them gave their views, and none of them had the slightest idea what to do about them. The president turned to the head of the CIA, the one man who technically would have some answers. He did of sorts, but they were insubstantial and certainly not enough to placate the Israeli prime minister.

Finally, the U.S. president locked his gaze on Mason from the far end of the room. He asked the admiral if he had a solution.

All eyes were on Mason.

He didn't speak.

Didn't need to.

Instead, he gave the tiniest of nods.

Admiral Mason was chauffeured in a bulletproof vehicle from the White House to the Pentagon. The car stopped in the secure underground parking lot; Secret Service agents escorted him through the vast labyrinth of corridors to his office and returned to their vehicles. Mason entered the large, oak-paneled room that he'd furnished in the design of an eighteenth-century man-of-war captain's quarters, and pressed a button on his desk's speakerphone. "I'm back. In here now. Both of you."

Mae Bäcklund and Rob Tanner entered without knocking and sat in leather armchairs facing their boss.

Tanner was in his early twenties and had the ready charm and confidence of a man who didn't have a care in the world. Courtesy of 661 C Street's Michael Anthony Salon, his auburn hair was designed in a medium-length ruffle that looked asymmetrical yet was strand perfect and fashioned to exude playboy nonchalance. His suits, handcrafted by Michael Andrews, were—the tailors of the bespoke salon often exclaimed—a pleasure to cut for a man whose physique carried no surplus fat because it was toned by a personal trainer. And his teeth and eyes shone because they were fixed that way. On the surface, Tanner was a fraud. He was, after all, a trust-fund baby; though unlike the majority of those who shared his financial ease into life, he had a Harvard-sharpened barrel-load of intellect. It wasn't enough. Tanner wanted to position himself to one day have power. And real power, he understood, rested on Capitol Hill and in the Pentagon. That was why he was in Mason's shitty office, sucking up rules and regulations and pocketing a government salary that barely made a dent in the bill for a bottle of *Krug Clos d'Ambonnay* fizz.

Tanner needed Mason to set him on a path where riches and cleverness would pale into insignificance compared to what could be achieved by a click of his fingers. The admiral knew that, and Tanner didn't care because if Mason didn't employ him, he'd have to employ someone just like him. Mason mentored Tanner, knowing that one day Tanner might try to stab him in the back. The trouble for Tanner was that nobody had ever successfully outwitted the admiral.

Mason needed his employees to have independent wealth. Those he'd previously employed had lacked that financial freedom and had quickly left to work in high-salary positions in investment banks and law firms. It had been a major irritation because Mason required subordinates who would serve out the duration of their terms and complete the tasks at hand. But that requirement came at a cost, and in the case of Tanner, it was having to endure the young Harvard grad's inflated ego and flippancy.

Mason had trawled Ivy League universities to find someone with Tanner's attributes. None of them suited him, and it was only by good fortune that the young man's resume landed on Mason's desk with a Post-it note on page one stating the guy wanted a job in government.

Bäcklund was different. She'd worked for Mason for half a decade and had seen other employees come and go. Only she remained because she was loyal, selfless, and adored Mason. It helped her work considerably that she was also calm, cerebral, and courageous in thought and conviction. Bäcklund was fully cognizant of the fact that Mason viewed her as the perfect counterbalance to the Machiavellian exuberance of the young bucks whom he'd handpicked to assist him and Bäcklund. Her usefulness in countering Tanner's excesses was no different. But that wasn't the sole reason why Mason had hired her. Mason had been a dear friend to her father, so much so that her dad had asked him to be his only child's godfather. Fourteen years ago, Mason was a ship's captain when her dad had asked Mason, "Do I walk from this?"

"Admiral, you're on your deathbed," Mason had replied.

"I expect better precision from you, Captain."

"Yes, sir," Mason had said. "I'll walk out of the hospital room. You'll float."

"I want angels and trumpets. Can you organize that for me?"

"I'll try my best, my friend."

"Want you to try harder on something—my daughter, Mae. Patty gone, she's all that's left."

"I don't have much money, but it will always be enough to look after her."

The admiral coughed, choked, nurses came, he ushered them away with his liver-spotted hands. Then he fixed his eyes on the man who had dark hair back then and a reassuring demeanor. "Mae's got money. Made sure of that. Man-to-man, I need . . ."

"I'll look after her."

"She'll tell you no man should be tasked to look after her."

"Then I'll tell her to look after me. It's not far from the truth." Mason bowed his head and held the admiral's hand as it grew cold. "I can't promise you angels."

Since her father's death, Bäcklund had considered Admiral Mason to be an uncle of sorts. Five years ago, she was twenty-seven, didn't need to work, and had just completed a PhD at Stanford. Mason took her out for a celebratory dinner wherein he asked her if she'd come to work as his assistant in a land-based Pentagon job he'd just been assigned to. At first she had declined, but Mason was canny and knew that part of her had aspirations one day to get into politics. He gave her sage counsel that before that day came, she could learn the ropes from the inside. He would teach her the ways of politics until such time as she was ready to broadside the ugliest natures of government and run for office. And teach he did. She respected the fact that he gave her no special dispensation because of who she was. On the contrary, Mason could be as withering in his comments to her as he was to Tanner. Only when they were alone would he soften and speak to her with a light touch and a paternal combination of admiration and concern for her well-being. Maybe Mason's role in her life would recede if she got hitched to a guy. Right now, that wasn't in the cards. On the rare occasions that men fleetingly entered her private life, the moments had made her feel sorrowful and unfulfilled. Finding the right guy was tough when you were an independent woman with a job that frequently shunted your brain into overdrive.

Bäcklund and Tanner were silent. Mason sat on the edge of his desk, and said, "Interesting meeting."

"President, Secretaries of Stuff, you." Tanner's smile broadened. "Who else was there?"

"Britain, France, and Israel." Mason patted his short, silver hair. "Their prime ministers, anyway, and via video link."

Bäcklund was motionless. "France equals pedantic legal jurisdiction. Britain equals meddling has-been. Israel equals rabid dog on a leash."

Mason eyed her with the look of a professor addressing a gifted but overly forthright student. "Perhaps I've been too long at sea to realize that the psyche of three countries can be distilled down to one sentence each."

It was Tanner who responded. "Perhaps you have, *sir*." He

was careful because Mason's intellect would crucify too much sarcasm. "Israel wants blood."

"Yes. Why?" Mason was very still, watching them like a killer who would turn on his captives if he or she gave the wrong answer.

Bäcklund put a cigarette in her mouth and left it unlit. "Israel kills a Hamas official last week; yesterday someone kills Israel's ambassador to Paris. Has to be Hamas; ergo two egos need to have a head to head in the locker room. Should we care?" She glanced at Tanner, wondering whether the man-boy seven years her junior would take her bait and make a crass remark. "Boys with dicks and toys. Right?"

"Yeah, right." Tanner tried to decide whether tonight he should finish writing his monograph on *God & Physics* or instead play Texas Hold 'Em poker with his pals. "Last time I checked, shit happens a lot in the desert. We shouldn't care."

Mason ran a finger along the crease in his trousers. "But we do care, don't we?"

"Not me." Tanner smiled.

Mason did not. "Then I'm in the company of a fool. *Think.*"

Bäcklund withdrew the unlit cigarette from her lips and looked at its sodden butt. "Escalation."

Tanner added, "Not just a few missiles lobbed into Gaza."

They took it in turns to articulate their thoughts at rifle-shot pace.

"It's an excuse."

"One Israel's been waiting for."

"Take revenge against Hamas."

"Big style."

"Invade Gaza . . ."

"The West Bank . . ."

"And . . ."

Mason nodded expectantly.

Bäcklund concluded, "Lebanon. Shit, this is a whole different story."

The admiral was pleased with his assistants because they'd nailed what the Israeli prime minister had said in the meeting. Israel believed the assassination of its ambassador gave it the legitimacy it needed to obliterate Hamas once and for all. And it had no problem invading two territories and one country to do so. "What position do you think France and Britain took?"

"You know the answer to that. You were at the meeting."

Mason said, "If I hadn't been there, I'd still know the answer."

Bäcklund placed the unlit cigarette in her jacket pocket, her craving for the cigarettes she so used to adore momentarily over. "They'll have made the obvious point that Israel has no concrete evidence that Hamas killed the ambassador, and in turn they'll say Israel doesn't yet have any legitimate ground in international law to start a ground offensive."

"Correct. Going to war on a hunch." Mason loosened the knot on his tie. "And what is our beloved president's stance?" This was to Tanner.

The young man was silent for three seconds. "He'll be urging Israel to be exercise restraint. But he'll also be worried that if he can't persuade Israel to hold fire, he's going to be in a political quagmire because if he doesn't show public support for Israeli actions, he's going to suffer big-time at the domestic ballot box."

"U.S. voters are not the only issue though I concede it is a relevant one." Mason looked out of the window at the manicured grounds beside his office and wondered if he'd be able to sneak in some Japanese Salix Hakuro-nishiki miniature trees in one of the flowerbeds. "The only solution for the president is to prove to U.S. voters that his decision to back or not back Israel is undeniably the correct one." Mason returned his attention to his employees.

Tanner asked, "You got an idea?"

"I do."

"You gonna share it with the president?"

Mason smiled. "I already have." His smile vanished. "And to everyone else present at the meeting. It's bought time. Israel's given me two months to make the idea work. If it doesn't, international law be damned as far as Israel's concerned. It will go to war with our without our blessing. People will have *opinions* about whether it's the right or wrong thing to do, but no one will know for a *fact* that it's the correct course of action because no one knows for a fact that Hamas killed the ambassador."

"And the Middle East will tear itself apart, before looking west." Bäcklund shook her head. "Anarchy. Bearded crazies foaming at the mouth and turning on us."

"Yes." There was a tinge of sadness in Mason's otherwise piercing cold blue eyes. "If my idea fails, the world should be wishing that I'd been a smarter man."

Tanner asked, "What is your idea?"

"We must get undeniable proof that Hamas did or did not conduct the Paris assassination." The admiral added, "My solution's being enacted right now. It's called Grey Site."

CHAPTER 6

Mosques were calling people to pray in Beirut, the amplified sounds nearly drowned out by the noise of traffic on the streets, the buzz of people going about their early-morning business, construction workers building and repairing buildings, and cargo vessels in the adjacent Mediterranean sounding their horns to warn other vessels that they were cruising slowly in and out of port amid a mist that still hadn't been burned out by the sun.

A tall man called Laith Dia—though that wasn't the name he'd used to enter Lebanon two days ago—ate a freshly baked za'atar croissant while standing in a doorway and watching not only a large derelict house, underneath which a newly constructed intelligence station had been established, but more importantly everything around the building. He was a paramilitary CIA officer. One of the men in the nearby subterranean complex was a colleague; the three other officers were respectively British MI6, French DGSE, and Israeli Mossad. Right now they were testing the newly installed electronic surveillance and intercept equipment. Laith was there to watch their back for twenty-four hours, trying to establish if there were any indications that people knew they were there. It was his last job for the CIA because, a week ago, he'd resigned from the Agency.

Though he was a big man with a striking visage, Laith blended in just fine. He looked like he was Lebanese, or certainly North African, and he was wearing clothes befitting an entrepreneur who was grabbing a bite to eat before heading off to his car dealership or dockland import and export business. It was a great time of day to do surveillance because people moving past him were bleary-eyed from drinking wine and smoking hookahs last night, and were oblivious to little else beyond getting to work and forcing their minds into gear. It would be easy to spot professional threats to the Western intelligence complex.

Laith sauntered along the street, taking another bite out of his breakfast while casually taking in his surroundings. The street was on the outskirts of Beirut, aligned with buildings that were residential and commercial, and was bustling with traffic and pedestrians. It was very different from how it had been during the preceding night when Laith had been here. Then, it had been almost deserted of people though the sounds of the city had been evident throughout his all-night vigil.

He saw an SUV stop. Two men got out and began walking along the street, one on either side of the route. Clearly, they were looking for something. They didn't look bleary-eyed. And though the young men looked similar to many of the pedestrians around them, they moved with vigor and purpose, showing no signs of having just dragged themselves out of bed after an evening of overindulging in the fine cuisines on offer in the city. After years of serving in the CIA and prior to that Delta Force, Laith knew the types. Still, they could just be innocents rather than Hamas terrorists who were looking for hostile intelligence officers who were spying on their activities.

Laith quietly spoke into his radio throat mic while watching the men. "May have something. Two men on foot. About one hundred yards from you. They're walking the street."

The MI6 officer in the underground intelligence office responded in Laith's earpiece. "Suspicious?"

"Hard to tell at this point."

The men were stopping people in the street, speaking briefly to them before moving on. Maybe they were asking directions. Or maybe they were inquiring as to whether the local residents had seen any recent activity wherein strangers had arrived and positioned themselves in their community. Perhaps these men were Hamas, but their intentions were benign. Though it was a terrorist organization, Hamas spent more time acting like Mafiosi—trying to get a grip on the streets of Beirut, policing it, doing business with locals, punishing them sometimes.

The men stopped outside the derelict house containing the intelligence complex.

Laith placed a hand over his concealed handgun, ready to run to the men if they went inside. "They're right outside your building. At stop."

"Shit!" The MI6 officer made no effort to conceal his unease. "But just two of them, right?"

"On foot, yeah." Laith glanced at the vehicle they'd earlier disembarked from. "But there's another three in the SUV. And that vehicle's following them at their pace, about fifty yards behind them."

Five potential terrorists versus five Western intelligence officers. But that wasn't the sum of it—what worried Laith and his colleagues was that a firefight would not only compromise the newly constructed intelligence station; it would also mean that he and his colleagues would somehow need to escape the Lebanon alive. And there was every probability that if the men he was watching were Hamas, they'd have reinforcements nearby.

"What are they doing?" The British officer sounded professional, yet tense.

"Just standing outside your building, looking around."

"Can you get to them if they enter?"

"Not sure because I'd have to take out the vehicle first."

Laith looked in the opposite direction. He saw another SUV at the end of the street. Again, the occupants looked different from locals. "Damn it. Another vehicle. Five more men."

"Coincidence?"

Laith answered, "I'm thinking not. But that doesn't mean they know you're here, or are looking for you."

The MI6 officer—a man called Edward, whom Laith had briefly met and who'd struck him as a cool-as-cucumber operator—said, "We're trapped in here! One route in and out. We won't stand a chance."

"Hold your nerve."

"They'll butcher us! I'd rather we took our own lives than let them get to us!"

888Laith saw the two men on foot get back into their SUV. It drove off at speed. The second SUV turned off the street into another road. They were gone.

Laith repeated, "Hold your nerve."

Rob Tanner walked across the vast external parking lot, paused by his vehicle while looking at the nearby Pentagon, and entered his car. It was midafternoon; all of the vehicles around him belonged to people who were still ensconced in the Pentagon, hard at work and wishing it was closer to 6:00 P.M. He used his vehicle's key to unlock the glove compartment and took out a cell phone that only one other man knew about. He powered it up and typed in the number that he'd memorized because the phone had no contacts list or anything else compromising within it. While it was ringing, he recalled the man who'd placed the phone in his hand, saying, "This is your first test. I hope I'm not making a mistake."

The man answered on the fourth ring but didn't speak.

Spots of rain hit the windshield, making Tanner worry about his hair when he'd walk back to his office. "I have news."

The man was silent.

"He's set up something called Grey Site. We need to meet."

Yesterday evening, Safa had watched a movie before getting into his new bed—one that contained sheets so lovely they felt as if they were an angel's hand encapsulating him and gently rocking him to sleep. The movie was made by Hollywood, and for most of the film there was only one actor—a man he'd never heard of. Since Safa's English was limited, his guardian had put on French subtitles. The American character was a courier man whose flight across the Pacific Ocean had crashed into the sea. He'd had to survive alone on a desert island for five years, his only companion a football on which he'd painted a face. To avoid death or the loss of his sanity, the American had finally decided to throw his life to fate and ventured away from the island on a raft. By pure luck, he was spotted and picked up by a cargo ship. Later, after receiving medical treatment and having his hair and beard cut so that he resembled the man he once was, he was flown back to the States. During that flight, he was given a glass of Coca-Cola with cubes of ice. The American could barely remember ice; it seemed remarkable and otherworldly to him.

Safa knew exactly how that felt.

He'd been on a desert island of sorts for all of his young life. Of course, he'd had glimpses of the outside world and had knowledge of what it contained. But it is not until you gaze upon these things in person, smell them, feel them, drink and eat them that you truly understand their wonder.

Since he'd arrived in France, there'd been so much to wonder at, almost to the point that everything around him was overwhelming. His guardian—the United Nations official who'd rescued him from Gaza—was mindful of this and careful with Safa's integration into the West. "Little by little," he'd told him over the preceding weeks. "We don't want your delicate mind overloaded."

Safa was educated by the UN man and lived in his home. It was a palace as far as the Palestinian boy was concerned though in truth it was big by the standards of most houses in France, it was no bigger than others that shared the same suburb of the city they were in. The house was tastefully furnished, had open fireplaces, books and oil paintings everywhere, wooden beams, ornate candles that were more often the source of light than electric bulbs, and an overall ambience of love, academia, warmth, and passion for locally sourced and well-cooked food. It was the home of a *seigneur*; a descriptive term that Safa had never heard of before but one that was explained to him by the guardian as a man who harked back to old Napoleonic times. A *seigneur* was privileged yet a true gentleman and leader who had compassion for all those who needed him. *Seigneurs* were not nobles; on the contrary, they desired to destroy the elitism of undeserved royal ascendancy. They were rebels but supremely powerful ones at that.

Safa had to be careful, the UN officer had told him upon arriving in France. Somehow, his guardian had managed to secure false papers for his charge, including a medical history. They were all in the name Safa though they had a different surname. But they were not enough to protect the boy since it was technically illegal for the real Safa to be in France. He needed a cover, his guardian had told him. If anyone asked, Safa's parents lived in Marseille, were French citizens, and had recently died. His guardian had legally adopted him. The UN official had given Safa many more details about his false background and current circumstances, and had made Safa memorize and recite these details over and over again until he was faultless.

Safa was in his bedroom when the UN man called, in French, from downstairs, "Safa, I need to speak to you."

Safa entered the open-plan kitchen-cum–living room, his favorite part of the house, and sat at the dining-room table. The UN officer brought him a cup of cocoa, and the smell of roasting chicken and rosemary wafted across the room from the large oven. Today was special. Since Safa had arrived in France, his guardian had taken him back and forth to private medical clinicians, particularly those who specialized in nutrition. Safa had been placed on a strict diet that allowed his body to slowly recover but didn't cause it to crash. He'd only been permitted small portions of meat and fish. But today, all bets were off. The doctors had given the boy the all clear to eat as much as his slim belly could cope with. And roast chicken was his meal of choice.

He sipped his cocoa, yet another addition into the repertoire of foods he was now permitted. Blessed God, it tasted so good.

His guardian sat opposite him and gently placed his hand on Safa's arm. "I've just received a call from one of my colleagues in Gaza. I'm so sorry, son. Your mother has passed away."

"Passed away?"

"Died."

Safa was unable to think clearly. He thought he should be crying, shaking, calling out to his beloved Mama. But the news came as no shock to him. Did this make him a bad boy, one with no heart? It all seemed so confusing because he had a huge heart.

His guardian must have sensed the conflict within him. "Listen carefully. I've traveled the world and seen more suffering than any man should. When people are surrounded by death, it has a different meaning. It's almost as if it's part of . . ."

"Life."

"Yes."

Safa took another sip of his cocoa. It didn't taste so good now. "How did she die?"

"The phrase *passed away* is apt. Because that's how she went. Peacefully. In her sleep. No pain."

"Is she with God now?"

"Yes, and your father is by her side." The UN official removed his hand from Safa's arm. "You have no one now. You must face up to that reality."

"I have you, sir."

"I am not family. Nor can I be."

"You look after me."

"I do, and I will do everything in my power to make sure

you're not sent back to that place." The guardian had concern written across his face. "Don't worry, Safa. I have connections. I know what I'm doing. And I will always look after you. But"—he adopted a stern tone though his expression was now one of true warmth—"I am a man of rules and principles, and it is a rule and principle that those in my household always eat a good meal, no matter whether we are elated or full of sorrow."

The meal was unlike any that Safa had eaten. His tummy was swollen afterward, though he didn't care. He'd consumed chicken with crispy skin, steamed fresh vegetables that were lightly glazed in unsalted butter, roasted parsnips, stuffing balls, all covered with a homemade gravy. It was food fit for kings, and that was exactly how Safa felt; or maybe he felt like a prince who dwelt with a good king.

They retired to the guardian's study. This was their evening ritual. Safa would always have a glass of water; the UN official would allow himself a small glass of port.

The guardian picked up a book from one of many on his shelves. It was red and looked old. "Charles Dickens was a very skilled English author. This book is written by him and is called *Hard Times*. I want you to close your eyes and relax. Don't worry that you can't understand the English words. Tonight, that's not what's important. Instead, I want you to listen to the rhythm of my voice, feel the musical flow of each sentence, and where possible remember how I pronounce some of the words. You are fortunate to speak French and Arabic. In sound, at least, the English tongue falls somewhere between those two languages."

He read for thirty minutes, regularly glancing at Safa in

case he opened his eyes or betrayed signs of not listening. But the boy looked entranced. In a calm and soothing voice, the guardian said, "Now we must turn our attention to your required medication and our daily reflection."

This was the part that the boy least enjoyed about his days in France, though the guardian was under strict orders from Safa's doctors to administer their prescriptions every evening. In truth, each day was getting easier and tonight the warm roast chicken in his tummy distracted him from fear.

The guardian opened a plastic box, withdrew from it a bottle of pills, tourniquet, and three syringes. Safa knew what to do. He swallowed the two pills handed to him, using the glass of water to wash them down, rolled up his sleeve, and held out his arm.

"That's my lad," said the guardian as he wrapped the tourniquet around Safa's bicep. He swabbed disinfectant over a prominent vein where upper arm met the underside of Safa's forearm, and eased the needle of the first syringe into Safa. "The first one's always the more painful one, isn't it?"

Safa nodded, his teeth gritted together.

"Just two more; smaller needles; almost no pain."

The medicine was administered. Many times Safa had asked what was in the pills and syringes; always his guardian had answered, but the names he used to describe the medicines were in Latin and so long that Safa could never remember them. Still, all that mattered was that his doctors and guardian could.

As always, he felt an almost instant tiredness overwhelm him; but there was also a sense that he was looking at himself from the other side of the study.

"It's the *outside-in effect*," the UN official frequently told him after his evening administrations of Safa's medicines. "It's the drugs' way of letting your mind watch your body get stronger each day. And in turn, they make your brain stronger because they give it reassurance that it's no longer in a weak vessel."

Safa rolled down his sleeve after Band-Aids were applied over the puncture wounds and the tourniquet removed.

The guardian positioned four mirrors next to each other on his study's desk. "Remember the drill?"

Safa swiveled in his chair to face the mirrors. "Yes. Though why so many mirrors this time?"

"We shall explore your question together." The guardian turned off the light so the room was in pitch-darkness, and stood behind Safa's back. He shined a flashlight at the mirror that was on the left. "Look at the reflection of light while we consider what we have learned and what we must still learn."

Safa nodded, his eyes transfixed, his body feeling as if it were floating.

"Today, we have a new tragedy to add to the others, do we not?"

"We do, sir."

"What is that tragedy?"

"The death of my mother."

"Correct." The guardian turned off the flashlight. "Is she gone?"

Darkness.

"Yes."

"Has the tragedy gone?"

"No."

The guardian illuminated the second mirror. "That's right. The tragedy does not want to die. Look at the light, Safa. What does it say to you?"

"Burning. Things burning in eternity."

"Hell?"

"Like Hell, but on Earth."

The guardian rested the flashlight on a shelf so that its beam remained focused on the mirror. He picked up another flashlight. "The mirror on the left has no light and holds the lives that have been unnecessarily extinguished. Your sister, mother, and father belong there. No light. Their deaths were avoidable."

"Avoidable." Safa knew that with certainty. "Avoidable."

"And the light that you can see reflected by the second mirror is the tragedy that we must allow to singe us with its flames. It must never be forgotten. But maybe one day it can be extinguished. Repeat that for me please."

"It must never be forgotten. But maybe one day it can be extinguished."

"Good. I want you to look at the third mirror while allowing the tragic light to continue to wash over you. Can you do this?"

Safa looked at the barely visible third mirror. "Is it bad? I don't know if I want it to be bad."

"Oh, no. This is the most wonderful thing in the world. It is a thing that forges a path into the future while correcting the past. The light I will shine on it will be bright and virtuous. But if you're not ready to see it, then we can do this during one of our subsequent daily sessions."

"I want to see it."

The guardian illuminated the third mirror. "Do you know what this is?"

Safa shook his head.

"It is you."

"Me?"

"The brightest light. Look at the mirror. It holds a reflection of you."

Safa stared at the mirror; its light would normally hurt his eyes and cause him to blink, but the drugs inside him made him calm, at peace, and dulled his nerves. He felt different though he always did after receiving his medication. And every morning thereafter, he felt his mind was changing into one of greater fortitude and clarity. He was evolving. "Me?" he repeated.

"You." The guardian's session was nearly at a close. There was so much more work to be done. Safa was nowhere near ready. But each daily session had to contain cautious little steps. Much like the way Safa's body had to be step by step carefully coaxed back to normal nutritional balance, so, too, his mind had to be gently manipulated to the place where it would never be the same again. The guardian owed that to the boy in his care; a child who could otherwise be traumatized by the horrors of his young life. "The mirror on the left with no light is beyond the control of you or anyone else. What has happened can never be undone. The mirror next to it burns with unbridled indignation and sorrow because it captures and holds tragedy. Only you can extinguish it, and only when matters have been put to rest. The third mirror is you. The brightest and purest light." He paused, wondering if he should stop now.

Safa asked, "The fourth mirror. Why does it have no light?"

"It does have light. But it is an evil one. I'm not sure you're ready to see what the mirror reflects."

"It reflects the bad in me?"

"There is no bad in you. The fourth mirror is the key to everything—the death of your family; the terrible circumstances of your childhood; the unnecessary deaths of so many others."

"What is it?"

"Gluttony, power, murder." The guardian hesitated. "We've never given that light a name, have we?"

"Never."

"Do you think it's time to do so?"

Safa was silent for a moment. That night, his caring guardian had taken him to a whole new level of well-being. Thank goodness the man had singled Safa out for a better life, where he could recuperate in the West. A child, still, but one receiving a very good education on what it took to be a balanced adult. "Yes, it's time."

The guardian turned off all flashlights. Then he illuminated the fourth mirror. "Don't be scared. But do be very cautious. Look at it."

The light was more intense than the others. Safa didn't like it; felt angry; wanted to smash the mirror though he wasn't sure why.

The guardian crouched next to Safa, his mouth close to the boy's ear, his eyes following his gaze toward the mirror. "It is a painful thing, is it not?"

Safa felt uneasy. "Gluttony, power, murder?"

The guardian whispered, "The embodiment of those nasty things in grown-ups who slaughter children."

"Where do those grown-ups live?"

"You must look to the two mirrors on the left. They can answer your question. It would be wrong for me to do so."

Safa thought about his dying parents; the way his younger sister had grabbed his arm while shrieking in pain, her expression terrified as she vomited blood onto her brother's raggedy shirt; the wails from Arab mothers in Gaza who served as belated air-raid-attack sirens as they ran down streets and alleys, their sons and babies no longer; and, worst of all, the starvation of his country. That was the insufferable horror; a rot that was surgically injected into a landmass; the life of people evaporating over months and years rather than seconds and days. "I have a word for the fourth mirror."

Safa's guardian placed his hand over the boy's shoulder. "But we must not run before we can walk. Our lesson is at a close. It is your bedtime now."

The guardian watched his young charge walk as if drunk toward his bed. In a few minutes he'd check up on him, make sure he had water next to his bed, was warm enough, and when he was asleep, he would gently pinch his flesh to check its growth. He'd never let the boy be without not only the essentials of life but also the tools to navigate his way through this world with success. The guardian owed him that. It was the duty of a man who called himself Thales.

CHAPTER 8

Beirut
Six weeks later

The CIA officer bade his three colleagues good night, watched them ascend the stairs toward the abandoned large house above, and shut the bombproof steel door. The air's musky scent caused him to pinch his nostrils with one hand while using the other to slam seven titanium bolts into place and turn keys in sophisticated locks. He walked back along the long and wide corridor that led to the four rooms in the underground complex while thinking it sucked to work the night shift alone in a place that resembled Hitler's subterranean Berlin bunker. The officer had operated in many hellholes and done so with exceptional composure and bravery. But this place gave him the jitters. Everything about it felt, looked, and smelled wrong. Particularly at night.

The bunker contained the most sophisticated communications-intercept equipment in the world, but the CIA technical guys who'd outfitted and reinforced the house's big wine cellar had seemingly not been overly concerned with ensuring there were enough lights in the complex. Day and night, the bunker was too shadowy because no natural light could get in; and the air was rank because air vents weren't allowed in the hermetically sealed fortress.

The steel door was the only portal to the outside world.

It was impossible to enter or exit the station by any other means.

And now that it was locked in place, the officer felt the weight of the slimy concrete walls, ceiling, and floor closing in on him. Above him was a city that he and his English, French, and Israeli partners spied on. Elements within the city would happily behead him and his MI6, DGSE, and Mossad colleagues if the complex was discovered. But on nights like this, the American operative often wondered if it would be preferable to take his chances in the city rather than sit, cornered, in a basement. His three foreign colleagues always felt the same way when it was their turn to be night-duty officer. Tonight they'd be relieved they were heading back to their hotel rooms rather than sitting alone on the cruddy furniture they'd bought at short notice from a local purveyor of flammable cheap shit.

Five weeks they'd been in here, one officer per room, for the most part with earphones on while listening to intercepts of Hamas cell phones, landlines, and e-mails, as well as more traditional bugs in situ. So far, all of it was giving the Agency nothing but insight on talk about God's peace and Real Madrid's soccer scores and the best way to debone and grill a goat. The officer sneezed as he walked along the corridor containing tall metal filing cabinets and an oil-powered electricity generator. He entered his room. All it needed was an oil lamp to make it look like the nighttime communications post

of a gaunt lieutenant on the front line of the Somme. Baby
flies emerged from a hole in the acrylic armchair the officer
slumped in as he attached his earpieces. One of the communications units' lights flashed, meaning a call was being made
to a Hamas target. The officer flicked a switch so he could
listen in. He heard code name Paganini talk in Arabic to
code name Stradivarius on their cell phones. The two senior
Hamas leaders were on this occasion not discussing mundane
matters. Instead, their tones were wary yet urgent, and their
words made the CIA officer's heart beat fast.

When the call ended, the officer dashed to the computer
terminal he used to send encrypted telegrams to the CIA
headquarters in Langley, Virginia.

Using two fingers, he typed fast.

PAGANINI HAS JUST CALLED STRADI-
VARIUS. THEY AND OTHER HIGH-
RANKING HAMAS LEADERS WILL BE
MEETING 4:00 P.M. LOCAL TIME TOMOR-
ROW TO DISCUSS THE "PARIS SHOPPING
TRIP." I HAVE COMPLETE ELECTRONIC
COVERAGE OF THE LOCATION OF THE
MEETING AND WILL ACTIVATE INTER-
CEPTION THIRTY MINUTES BEFORE THE
MEETING. PAGANINI SAID THAT "THALES"
HAD CONTACTED HIM AND TOLD HIM TO
BE VERY CAREFUL BECAUSE THE AMERI-
CANS MIGHT BE WATCHING HIM. I HAVE
NO IDEA WHO THALES IS. ANY INSIGHT?

Langley responded in less than a minute.

EXCELLENT. REPEAT, EXCELLENT. THIS IS GOLD DUST. WE WILL IMMEDIATELY INFORM MI6, MOSSAD, AND DGSE. THE MEETING WILL GIVE US THE EVIDENCE WE'VE BEEN LOOKING FOR. THALES HAS NO MEANING TO US.

The officer breathed out slowly and felt his shoulder muscles relax. Admiral Mason's initiative six weeks ago to establish the intelligence station in Beirut had been the right call although everyone involved in his initiative had always realized it was a long shot. And so much was at stake if the station couldn't deliver. But its establishment paid off. Tomorrow's meeting would prove whether Hamas killed the Israeli ambassador to France or not. But that wasn't the only reason the officer felt relieved. He and his three colleagues had been going mad cooped up in the station. They were desperate to leave the complex for good.

An intelligence complex that carried the name Grey Site.

The American withdrew his handgun and stripped it down to its working parts. After he cleaned each part, he reassembled the weapon and placed a fresh clip of bullets in the pistol. He waited for his colleagues to arrive in the morning.

About the Author

As an MI6 field officer, **MATTHEW DUNN** acted in deep-cover roles throughout the world. He was trained in all aspects of intelligence collection, deep-cover deployments, military unarmed combat, surveillance, and infiltration. During his time in MI6, Dunn conducted approximately seventy missions—all of them successful. He is the author of *Spycatcher*, *Sentinel*, *Slingshot*, *Dark Spies*, and the forthcoming *The Spy House*, all featuring Will Cochrane. He lives in England.

www.matthewdunnbooks.com
www.witnessimpulse.com

Discover great authors, exclusive offers, and more at hc.com.